DARKEST HOUR

JACK HUNT

DIRECT RESPONSE PUBLISHING

Dedication

For my family.

Prologue

I understand now.

I mean, why they did it.

Someone should keep a record — not of what happened or how few survived but as a warning to future generations. Never could I have foreseen it ending this way, nor imagined that any of this was even possible.

Ignorance got us here; failure to act sooner was our downfall.

I don't want you to make that mistake. We can't allow it.

In the event of my death these words will live on, forever etched into stone as a message to those still fighting. If you're reading this now, just know you're not alone.

Though few, pockets of resistance still exist.

It's getting harder to know who to trust. They've adapted, evolved and become smarter but there is still hope. As long as there is breath in your lungs, never give up.

Far too many gave their lives so we can live.

This is our world, our country and our home, and you must defend it at all costs.

I scrawled furiously against the Cutler sandstone capped by harder Moenkopi sandstone and caked in a red mud curtain. The words, bright and clear, the images easier to grasp than the Sego Petroglyphs. Once done, I stepped back to admire the handiwork. Each message would tell a tale. Each engraving would paint a picture.

I breathed in deeply and closed my eyes.

Nine hundred feet up in the air, standing upon the soaring fin of Titan Tower, amongst a maze of pinnacles, minarets, gargoyles, spires and strangely shaped rock formations, I soaked in the golden sunrise spreading over the towering depths of Fisher Towers in Utah.

What a beautiful sight.

This is where it all began.

This started it all.

The sun, the flare, the change in trajectory, and them.

A hard wind blew against my skin, I closed my eyes feeling its warmth before opening to a world changed by evil. Though the buildings would decay, this message would remain.

I stepped up to the edge and peered over.

At one time, teetering on the edge of the unknown terrified me but that was weeks ago, long before this, before them, before I witnessed the horror that cost so many lives. So am I scared? Of course, but this is a walk in the park compared to what lies below. Again, I turned and moved far enough back before looking towards the horizon. I breathed in deeply before firing forward, legs pounding the ground like pistons as I hit my stride. The sound of blood rushed in my ears, the cries of the fallen tore at my heart and his words echoed as the tower fell away.

"Ready to die?"

Chapter 1

Moab, Utah

A bright fireball lit up the starry sky. Hissing, crackling and popping like a hundred fireworks erupting before the earth-shaking sonic boom. The explosion was sudden then the shaking stopped. They stared at each other. A wild look of surprise. Shooting stars were often seen but nothing had crashed nearby. One of the four eighteen-year-old guys craned his neck over the edge of Parriott Mesa, the largest mesa guarding the entrance to Castle Valley. From the highest point they had a clear view of Arches, Castle Valley and the La Sal Mountains. They'd woken up early that day and driven over to Parriott from Moab. It was one of the many jump sites they had in the central heart of the most adventurous area of Utah. They were lying on their sides, drinking beer and shooting the breeze when it all began. The nearby crash rattled the sandstone walls like thunder, except the sound was more akin to the earth splitting in two.

"What the hell was that?" JT muttered as one by one they scrambled to their feet.

They stood there focusing on the fiery glow in the distance. Excitement and curiosity soon got the better of them.

"Only one way to find out," Blake Davis replied, reaching for his pack. "Gear up, boys."

"But what about the mats, the brews, and—"

"Just get in your suit," Blake hollered at JT.

They'd planned on sleeping there the night and then wingsuit BASE jumping early in the morning once the sun began to rise, but this was too good to pass up. Blake glanced at his watch, it was already a little after one in the morning. Up at an elevation of over six thousand feet, nothing but the sound of the wind could be heard. With summer temperatures soaring in the high eighties, and nothing more than their rigging gear and thin roll-up mats to sleep on, they were roughing it. But that's how they liked it; nothing but earth beneath their feet and a starry sky above.

Declan and Zane crunched empty cans of cheap beer beneath their boots and hooted and hollered as one by one they slipped into their wingsuits, and prepared to leap into the darkness. They had grown up in Moab, and the outdoors had become a way of life. They had their hands in a little of everything: motocross, BASE jumping, climbing, slack lining, skydiving, river rafting and zip lining. They did it all. There were few days they weren't out tearing up the sky, or soaking in the sights.

"Light 'em up," Blake said.

The wingsuits flickered to life casting a cool blue glow over the lightweight material. It was all the rage now as jumpers pushed the envelope and ventured into the risky act of wingsuit diving at night. The LEDs made it a lot easier to see each other; and besides, it was one hell of a sight. Videos of their flights had racked up a crazy amount of views online and had not only garnered the attention of the tight-knit community but the admiration of their peers.

Blake breathed in deep, a smile dancing on his face.

Even now after all the jumps they had done, he still felt the rush of excitement as he peered over the edge. He tossed back the rest of his beer before tossing it out and waiting to hear it bounce off the canyon wall.

They flipped down their visors and did a final gear check. He made sure they could hear one another over the comms unit that was custom fitted into each of the helmets.

He tapped JT on the shoulder.

"You ready?"

"Always."

Declan and Zane butted their helmets together and gave a thumbs-up.

Blake stretched out his arms as a surge of exhilaration and fear mixed like a sweet cocktail. It never changed no matter how many times he jumped — it was an addictive feeling, an adrenaline rush that drew millions from around the world every year to Moab.

Whether it was jumping, climbing or skydiving, there was nothing else like it.

"See you at the bottom," he yelled before pushing off the edge and watching the earth rush up to meet him. Nothing compared to those first three seconds. It was damn near perfect, a true spiritual experience.

As he plummeted towards the ground, the cool wind washed over and under his suit creating a cushioning effect. A few slight adjustments and he veered his way through the Mars-like landscape of wild mud curtains and gnarled and twisted rock knobs.

Few dived at night, for obvious reasons. It was risky. The chances of things going wrong only increased when visibility was low. The air was thick with dust. A sudden shift in wind could prove deadly. If he hit one of the stone walls that rose like fingers, he knew it was game over. What they were doing was dangerous, reckless even, but that's why they did it. Life was about pushing the envelope, and anything less was playing it safe.

Zane hollered over the comms. "This is spicy."

"Hell, yeah!"

It was hard to hear as turbulent wind lashed at his helmet. The muscles in his legs tightened as he kept them stretched wide to prevent the tail wing from flapping. He turned his head to the side in time to see JT do a barrel roll. To the right, Zane moved through a front loop. It wasn't in them to do anything less. There was something to living life on the edge, to being seconds away from death's door. No drug could give them that high.

They shot through the air like missiles heading towards the crater of flames. He was closing in on ninety miles per hour. Whatever had split the atmosphere must have burned up on entry as he could still see a trail of dust and cloud streaking the night sky. As they got closer, he could see several small pits of fire surrounding the impact zone.

It has to be a meteor shower, he thought.

It took seconds to drop from six thousand to three thousand feet.

Blake reached around, pulled the ripcord and deployed his pilot chute. The suspension lines stiffened, and he felt himself being yanked up. After he grabbed the toggles, he made sure he was clear of the other three as he veered east of the crash site.

The comms unit crackled as their voices came over, loud and clear.

"Damn, this is one for the books," JT muttered.

"We will be famous."

They'd visited the sites of smaller meteors that had crashed many years ago but not one this large. It had to have been as wide as one school bus. As they got closer, he could feel the heat coming off it. He focused in on a patch of earth that was a safe distance away.

Dirt rose to meet him, he bent his knees and pulled on the toggles to slow his descent as he prepared to do a two-stage flare. When he was close to fifteen feet from the ground he brought the canopy to level flight and bled off forward speed. He leaned forward pulling harder on the toggles until he hit the ground and broke into a slow run.

The chute settled to the ground behind him and he unclipped.

He flipped up the visor and breathed in. The air was hot.

None of them rushed forward, instead they kept their distance.

JT whipped out his cell phone and started recording.

"This shit is going online ASAP. We will have the media swarming us and…"

Blake slapped his arm down. "Don't put it online, sell it to the media. We'll give them an exclusive."

"No one will believe we were first to see it."

"Of course they will." Blake stepped into frame as JT continued to focus on the cup-shaped depression. It looked like the orifice of a volcano with all the fire coming out of it. Even if they had wanted to see inside, they couldn't get close to the rim, as it was too hot.

"My name is Blake Davis. As you can see no one else is here except us. We've just arrived at a meteor impact site. This will be headline news today and the online world will blow up, so I wanted you to know who found it first." He motioned for each of them to get into frame. JT turned the camera on them as they slung their arms around each other's necks and grinned at the camera. Blake then directed JT to focus his attention on the crater. "That's it, zoom in. Get some good footage."

They stood there for a good ten minutes taking it all in.

Blake scanned the perimeter and noticed it was covered in small chunks of rock, some of which were still on fire. Zane went over to pick one up and he yanked him back.

"Don't touch that, you idiot. You'll burn your skin off."

"No, he won't," Declan said. They turned to find him tossing a chunk of it around. He wiped some of the black dust off the top. "Check out the color in this. Here." He tossed it to Blake and he caught it to prevent it striking him in the forehead. He scowled back, his mouth forming a thin line. Turning it over in his hand, for a few seconds he stared at the unusual colors peeking through the charred crust. He was about to toss it when he felt a sharp pain course through his hand causing him to drop it.

"What the hell...?"

His palm was bleeding, and his arm throbbed. Almost instantly he felt unwell, like he was coming down with a stomach bug. He got this intense burning sensation in the back of his throat and for a few seconds his vision became blurred.

"You okay?" TJ asked.

He brought a hand up to his head and staggered a little.

"Come on, let's get out of here before the cops show up."

Chapter 2

5 Days Later

We drove the grueling thirteen-hour journey to Moab over two days. My mother and I took turns driving while my younger brother Zac slept in the back of the beat-up station wagon hauling a mini U-Haul trailer.

It was meant to be a fresh start. A time to leave behind the past and have a clean slate, she said. By that she meant, forgetting that our father hadn't survived a drunk driving incident a year earlier.

I got it. I did. It was painful.

But I couldn't help see the move as nothing more than an attempt at escaping from a past that none of us could ever escape. We would carry that memory for the rest of our lives. Our mother wasn't just forcing us to leave behind every friend we'd ever known, including my longtime girlfriend, but disrupting our education. I still had one year of school, Zac had three; it wasn't meant to be like this. None of it was.

"Cheer up, guys, you will love it."

She switched on the radio and began singing along with some crappy pop tune, in a failed attempt to lift our spirits. It wasn't working. Neither of us said anything. I glanced out the window as we veered off I-70 and made our way onto the final stretch of US-191 that fed into our future.

Near the southern edge of Grand County in eastern Utah was the small city of Moab. Hell, it was barely a city, more of a town. Its population? Only 5,242, though according to our mother that figure rose every weekend as thousands of people from around the globe traveled to take in the massive red rock formations in Arches National Park and Canyonlands, and ride the swirling rapids of the Colorado River. Still it was a blip on the map in my eyes, a stark difference to Rapid City, South Dakota, which has over 74,000 residents.

"It doesn't even have a Walmart. I mean, what town doesn't have a Walmart?" Zac muttered while playing away on his handheld PlayStation.

She eyed him in the mirror. "Okay, I admit, you aren't going to find any big box retailers here but that's the beauty of it." She brought down the window and breathed in the desert air. "Just breathe that in."

"I think I'm choking," Zac joked.

"Oh, you guys, you just wait and see."

Our mother had a bit of a wild spirit to her. Most would say she was a hippie. She had long dark hair, wore one too many necklaces and bracelets, and most days opted for a tie-dye dress and sandals. She'd grown up in Moab but never gone beyond its border until the age of eighteen when she moved out east to study before landing a position as a dispatcher with the Rapid City Police Department. That's where she met our father. Four years later they were married. From what I can remember, they were good for one another. He brought a stability that she wanted but refused to admit, and she kept him from living life too rigid.

We had it good for a while but that was all swept away in one night.

Eighteen years on the job, he'd stared down the barrel of a gun countless times but it wasn't a bullet that ended it — it was a drunk driver. Yeah, that was a tough pill to swallow.

Now, we were on our way to live with gramps, a guy who was even crazier than our mother. Because of my age, she said I could have remained in Dakota but it would have meant leaving Zac, and her, and after all we'd been through? It wasn't going to happen. Not now. Even though it had been a year since his death, the pain was still fresh, even if our mother tried to cover it up with a smile.

Sunlight reflected off the front windshield and I squinted towards the horizon.

Our mother beamed. "Just check out that view."

Red rock rose either side of US-191 which carved its way down into the heart of Moab. Though others marveled at its natural beauty, and must have seen it as representing adventure — to me, it was a distraction.

"What's there to see? It looks like Mars," I commented.

"Might as well be," Zac said, sulking in the back.

"Listen, guys, I don't want either of you causing problems with grandpa. He's going out of his way to put us up. Now you know he's set in his ways. He has a certain order to how he lives, so I would appreciate it if you refrained from making sarcastic remarks."

Zac piped up. "I don't see why we have to stay there."

"It's just until I can find us a place. Two weeks, a month at the most."

"Right." He rolled his eyes. "He wouldn't still be wearing that silver foil hat on his head, would he?"

She let out a gentle chuckle. "If he is, don't you dare say anything."

Gramps was the weirdest guy I'd ever met. Our grandmother had passed away eight years ago. When I was younger, our mother would bring us out to see her parents. Though my memories of him were foggy, I could recall him wearing a silver foil hat, and running some local radio station that covered conspiracies, cryptids and paranormal events.

"Besides, I think you'll love the trails out here, Logan. Mountain biking, hiking, river rafting, off-roading, you name it, this place has it. It's an outdoor enthusiast's playground, a place you'll eventually come to see as home."

She was overselling us on the place. We both knew she was hyping it up as the next best thing since sliced bread, all in an attempt to feel better about deciding to move. How could anyone fault her? She was doing the best she could under the circumstances.

We exchanged a few more comments about different events in Moab, the kind of outdoor activities available, and then that was pretty much it. I continued to soak in the sight of the arid landscape. It was breathtaking; there was no denying that. Mostly sandstone with a healthy smattering of green trees, it wasn't South Dakota but then again there wasn't much like where we'd come from. My father had drilled into me from an early age the benefits of hunting and fishing. It was more than a sport to him, it was a way of life. Though I was too young to own a firearm, my father had taken me along with him to the firing range and shown me how to shoot. I could still remember his words.

"Equal height, equal light."

He was referring to the knife-edge across the top of the front and rear sights.

We passed by a Motel 6, gas stations, a fossil shop, car washes and several flea-ridden inns. At the edge of the road, worn-out weathered signs advertised going out of business sales, and discounts. There were several small clothing stores, greasy fast-food joints, diners and a host of services offering adventure tours, camping equipment and rentals. After we veered off to our left, the houses began. All of them were spread apart, clapboard and stone, some modern, others aged.

We continued heading south. It was another three

miles before we turned left into a sprawling neighborhood of clapboard homes set back from the road, each one tucked behind a cluster of trees.

Slowly it became more familiar.

Barely visible from the weeds, and thick underbrush, an old rusted mailbox with gold lettering on the side displayed gramps's address: 1789 South Highland Drive. The tires crunched over gravel as we turned in and weaved our way up the narrow driveway full of potholes until we came out into a clearing just in front of the home.

I pushed out of the vehicle, arched my back to work out the tension. Mom killed the engine, and it continued to tick. The afternoon sun beat down on us as we stood in the middle of the driveway staring at the ranch-style, one-story home. If it had been a few miles to the north, it would have been nestled in Castle Valley. It was a run-down white clapboard home with paint that was chipped away. The roof was covered in old brown shingles that curled up at the edges. One window had been patched up with some cardboard. There were four steps that went up to a dark brown porch with one rocking chair. The surrounding landscape was dry. Peaked mountains and a desert valley framed the home giving it an almost picturesque view. Out front, wind chimes hung from a dead tree. They jangled in the light breeze. Sagebrush and various wildflowers surrounded the perimeter of the residence.

"Home sweet home," mom said.

Our mother reached into the car and beeped the horn. A few seconds later a brittle screen door swung open and out he shuffled, hunched over and looking like he had one foot in the grave. His hair was wispy, white and braided like Willie Nelson's. He even had a red skull bandana and cowboy hat to match.

"Sage, ah, my girl, you're here at last."

"Hey Dad."

Our mother hurried over and gave him a big hug before he stepped back and took a look at her. "Have you lost weight?"

She grinned. He might as well have told her she had won the lottery. Our mother wasn't fat, but she had gained a few pounds since the funeral. Grief could do that. He gave her another hug, then eyed us over her shoulder. His beady eyes narrowed, and I got this sense he wasn't too keen on having two rambunctious guys tearing around his property and eating him out of house and home.

"Logan, my boy. Why, you have grown since I last saw you."

"Hey Gramps," I said heading over and getting an awkward hug from him. He smelled like dank weed and coffee. "You still running that radio show of yours?" I said, trying to break the ice.

"You bet. Which gives me a great idea, I'll have you two on as guests next week."

Zac grimaced.

I raised a hand and waved. "Ah that's okay," I mumbled, hoping he'd forget. The last thing I needed being new to the neighborhood was gaining a reputation as the town loon. Fitting in would be hard enough as it was. He broke away and smothered Zac in a bear hug while I continued to root around in the back of the U-Haul for our belongings.

I carried into the house a stack of boxes and came to a grinding halt. It was like a hoarder's heaven. Clutter everywhere. Anything and everything was clogging up every square inch of the hallway and living room off to the right. Antique oddities from around the globe, bearskin rugs and a large collection of crystals, no doubt once belonging to our mother, adorned the hardwood floor. The walls were a light brown and curtains dark blue. If the curtains hadn't been open, it would have looked dreary. There wasn't a splash of color to be seen except from a few of the crystals. It was rustic and had four bedrooms on the main floor. The kitchen was a modest size with cream linoleum that was uneven, and there was a ratty-looking bathroom at the far end of the hallway.

I motioned with my head to the crystals. "Those yours,

Mom?"

"No, those were your grandmother's. She was the one who got me into that," she said carrying in two suitcases.

"Where should we put our stuff?" Zac asked while he clutched a basketball under one arm and a duffel bag in the other hand.

"I've got both of you down in the basement," grandpa said pointing a gnarled finger towards a locked door. He shuffled over and pulled off a set of keys from his belt and unlocked a padlock.

"Why's it locked?" Zac asked.

I leaned in and whispered in his ear. "It's where he keeps all the dead bodies."

Zac snorted and reluctantly headed down the narrow staircase into the dimly lit unfinished basement. I thought the upstairs was a shambles, the basement looked worse.

"Where's my bed?"

"Below the sink."

"What?"

Grandpa laughed. "You thought I would leave you two

peckerwoods down here, didn't you?"

Yep, he still had a weird sense of humor.

I raised an eyebrow. Zac dropped the box and moved over to the far wall and played around with some of the knobs on a large electronics unit. It was covered in a thin layer of dust.

"Hey don't touch that," grandpa said slapping his hand. "That's expensive CB radio gear."

"Doesn't look like you use it."

"I make use of it every day."

"Hey Gramps, you know there is something called the internet, right?" I muttered.

"Internet?"

"Yeah, the World Wide Web, CNN, YouTube, porn, you know, the staple diet of every American."

He grumbled. "Like that will help when the world comes to an end." He slung a thin yellow sheet over the equipment. "You youngsters don't know what to do with yourself unless you have your face in a phone or are playing those damn games. In my day…"

And that was that, he was off rambling about how life was much better in his day and how teens used to be creative with their time. Zac and I exchanged a confused look and headed back upstairs.

It took several trips to unload the U-Haul. My mother caught me sighing as I sat in the back of the empty trailer and brushed off the dust and grime of the day from my pant legs.

"You can buy another when you get a job here."

She was referring to the Kawasaki dirt bike I sold so that for the first few months I wouldn't have to rely on her for money while I searched for a job.

"I know."

"Maybe you can even get a Jeep this time. Everyone has them here, ain't that right, Dad?"

He grunted. "What? Not me. I can't be doing with that newfangled technology. No, not me, if people need to find me they can show up at the house."

"I said Jeep, not cell phone."

"Oh, yeah, I don't have one of those either," he

muttered walking away with the last box.

Off to the side was his beat-up, 4x4 with rust holes in it, which looked like something from the 1970s. Heading back into the house, gramps told us which rooms were ours, and what rooms we weren't to go in.

"I'm taking that room," I said before Zac could get in there. It was the south bedroom that gave a sweeping view of the mountains whereas the north side had little to look at except grandpa's chicken pen, and an old faded white garage off to the right.

"C'mon. I've got way more stuff than you."

"I need an area for my weights."

He was about to argue the point but just dropped his head and turned.

"Zac." He looked back. I motioned with my head. "Go ahead."

"You sure?"

"Just move your stuff in before I change my mind."

I could have been an ass about it but I knew he'd taken the loss of our father far worse than I had. Though I missed him, and it was the worst pain I'd ever experienced, our relationship had been strained in the year leading up to his death. We'd butted heads over what I wanted to do. He'd always had these grand ideas of me joining the military or police, but that just wasn't my thing. I respected what he did, but I had aspirations to do something else — I just couldn't pin down what that something was, and it annoyed the heck out of him. So I guess in his eyes it meant I would do nothing with my life.

I tossed a box on the bed and gazed up at the large African mask on the wall. It was freaky looking and certainly the first thing that would be tossed out.

There was a gentle rap at the door as I unpacked my belongings.

"Spoke with grandpa. He said there is an ATV rental shop in the north end of town that is hiring. Maybe after school tomorrow, you can drop by there. Who knows, perhaps if you get hired they'll loan you a vehicle to get around in." She noticed there was an open box with

LIVING ROOM scribbled on the side. "Oh, that shouldn't be in here."

I grabbed it up and spotted a photo of all of us inside, a snapshot of better days. Long before life got in the way. I handed it over and she took it out. "Why don't you put it on the side table?"

I hesitated before taking it. "Sure."

She ran a hand around the back of my head. "It will work out, Logan. I have a good feeling." As she left the room, I placed the photo down, gazed out the window and breathed in deep. *I hope so, I really do.*

* * *

Grand County was the only high school in Moab. It had a grand total of 450 students, prior to our arrival. Our mother had given us the rundown that morning over breakfast. Compared to the nearly 2,000 students back in Rapid City, it could be said the chances of blending in unnoticed were slim to none. I'd woken up late that morning, even though according to mother, gramps had already called out to us seven times. Thing was, it had been hard to fall asleep. It wasn't just the fact it was a new place. Moab was a hell of a lot hotter than South Dakota and the house didn't have air-conditioning, only old ceiling fans covered in dust. It had taken me the better part of three hours to fall asleep and by the time I woke up I was exhausted. A warm band of light peeked through the blinds and the daunting fact that all eyes would be on us made my stomach churn.

The new kids. We might as well have had a sign around our necks that said, stay clear of us.

When I made it downstairs, Zac was sitting at a circular pine table covered in newspaper and greasy mechanical parts. Gramps said he would clear it away the day before but he hadn't. Zac's eyes closed as he chewed on toast, while mom washed dishes because grandpa didn't believe in owning a dishwasher. It was one of the many weird things he couldn't accept.

Breakfast that morning was quiet, except for the drone of a small TV. A news anchor was discussing solar flares while mother gave a spiel about Grand County being a popular high school.

"Popular? It's the only one," Zac replied. "Maybe you can just homeschool us."

"Ah, you'll be fine," she said. "I'll drop you off and…"

I leaned against the dull white cabinets that looked as if they'd been installed in the late 1960s. I was chugging back coffee, trying to get my caffeine fix.

"Mom, you think I can take the car?" I asked, hoping to avoid any further embarrassment. Thoughts of her shouting out "I love you" through the passenger window as students looked on made me sick. *One year. That's all you've got left. Then you're out — a free man.* Hell, I was a man. In some countries in the world teens were done with school and in the workforce by age sixteen. I'd just turned eighteen.

"But I need to visit the real estate office today, and…"

"You can use my truck," grandpa said walking into the room with a bowl full of cereal and wearing nothing more than a pair of white Y-fronts and a dressing robe.

"Dad, cover up."

"It's my home. I'll do what I like," he grumbled.

She rolled her eyes as he poured out his second cup of coffee and turned up the TV. Mother tossed me the car keys. "Logan, don't ding it and make sure—"

"I'll take good care of it. Don't you worry."

"Shhh, keep it down, I'm trying to hear this," grandpa said before turning up the volume.

"… and we start with some breaking news this hour. As mentioned in previous broadcasts, residents of Moab, Utah, saw a bright fireball light up the night sky five days ago. It's been confirmed that a meteorite exploded as it entered earth's atmosphere causing a meteor shower. Eyewitnesses reported that several blasts left behind long trails of smoke in the air. We now go to David Rogers who is at the impact zone. David, can you tell us what is going on there?" The TV footage changed to a guy close to a large crater. *"Hi Susan, okay, well imagine you are out taking in the night sky, everything is peaceful and calm and suddenly a massive fireball appears out of nowhere in the sky. You're thinking to yourself, is this a plane crash or a nuclear attack or a UFO?*

Well, for the one that appeared over the skies of Utah, we can confirm that this was a meteor shower. Fortunately it wasn't large, no one was harmed, and it landed just northeast of Moab. Now what we know from officials and eyewitnesses, is that there was a series of explosions, probably around four or five when the meteor entered our atmosphere and then molten hot debris rained down over the landscape. One witness said it sounded like thunder. It rattled windows, and… well… Obviously this caused a lot of panic, concerns and 911 calls." He pressed a finger into his ear. *"Now we obtained amateur footage of the crash site on the night of impact. You'll recall us playing this a few days ago. This was sent in by some local teens who were in the area. You should see that now on your screen."*

I squinted as a photo showed up on the screen of four young guys doing a selfie with the impact site behind them. It switched to some footage before the fires went out, then went back to the news anchor.

"So as you can see, a lot has changed since that night. Gone are the fires that were shown in the video. What we

have been able to gather is that a solar flare was responsible for the change in trajectory of multiple meteors. The Space Weather Program said the West Mountain Observatory had been monitoring several that should have passed by the earth but changed course due to a sudden flare. Now for those who are unfamiliar with what a solar flare is, in laymen's terms, it's when giant balls of gases erupt and spit out bursts of energy. We're told this occurs all the time, and usually these don't affect us on a large scale, however, concerns have been raised this week that it may have only been the precursor to a major solar storm heading our way."

"Sounds dangerous," Susan said.

"It is. U.S. astronomer Martin Brighton, who has monitored some of the less powerful solar storms over the past decade, said modern society would be underprepared to handle a large-scale storm."

That's when Susan cut in again.

"So what would we be looking at in terms of damage and scale?"

"Well that's the thing, Susan, a large solar storm can have

devastating effects on satellites, mobile phones, vehicles, internet, the banking systems and all manner of technology that is powered by the electrical grid. Essentially it would be catastrophic."

Mother came over and went to turn off the TV but grandpa slapped her hand. "Don't you dare. I'm listening to this."

"Dad, it's just fear-based nonsense."

"That's what they all say until it happens," he shot back spitting cereal over his wrinkled lips.

"Hey Gramps, is it common for the CDC to show up to every meteor site?" I asked, looking inquisitively at the various figures in white hazmat suits.

"Who knows what that thing is contaminated with?" he replied.

A video then played showing a close-up of the sun, and massive arching bursts of fire as David continued to explain. *"Now the best way to understand how this works is if you think of a solar storm in terms of a gun going off. The initial muzzle flash you would see is what could be referred* to as the solar flare, the bullet that would follow would be a coronal mass ejection, known as a CME. This CME is a cloud of plasma and energy that would strike the earth with such force it would destroy electronics and fuse conductive wires, and no doubt take out satellites in orbit too. Now the closest we have come to a big one in recent years was a solar storm in July 2012, but fortunately that didn't hit the earth. Had it done so, large parts of society could have been without power for months, even years. Prior to the 2012 storm, the earth has been hit by a few small ones, one of which caused the 1989 Quebec blackout, another in 2003 in Sweden, another in 2005, however they didn't even come close to the largest recorded storm which was the Carrington Event of 1859. This is when a massive solar flare and CME struck the earth and destroyed much of the telegraph networks in Europe and North America."

"And so in light of the recent flare, what are the odds of that occurring again, David?"

"Good question. Well, while solar astronomers can't give us an exact date or know exactly what causes flares, *they know the sun's power increases every eleven years but that doesn't mean it couldn't happen sooner. The one in 2012 was the closest we have come to the power of the Carrington Event."*

"So as long as we don't get a CME, we should be fine?"

"Somewhat. Flares, depending on the size, can cause static on your radio and TV, create aurorae lights and create power outages like we saw in 1989. That also explains why some folks experienced a loss of power on their cell phones five days ago."

"So can they predict if we will get this big solar storm?"

"Yes, no, maybe. There are conflicting reports about this. It has already created several heated debates. I hate to say it, Susan, but a large solar storm could cause an apocalypse on earth within a matter of twelve hours' warning."

He got this smile on his face as if he thought it was a big joke. It didn't exactly add to his credibility. No wonder people didn't take this stuff seriously.

Susan's eyes widened. "Twelve hours? That's it?"

"From what we have been able to gather, yes. Like I said,

Susan, there have been a lot of debates over this. According to the U.S. consortium led by NASA, they proposed to develop an early-warning system for these kinds of hazardous storms years ago. Had this been in place it would allow up to a five-day warning, which would give people more time to prepare. However, discussion on this took place back in 2012, that's over five years ago and there still doesn't appear to be anything in place. So your guess is as good as mine. Twelve hours might be all we have."

I shook my head and put my crumb-covered plate into the sink. The news continued to play out in the background, spewing more fear and uncertainty into the minds of Americans. It never changed.

"We're going to be late, c'mon, Zac." I scooped up my bag, snatched another piece of buttered toast, stuffed it between my teeth and gave Zac a tap around the head to slap him out of his morning daze.

* * *

"You want to slow down?" Zac said. "I want to get there alive."

I eased off the gas not even realizing how fast I was going. I didn't want to end up late and walking in while a class was in session. We would already have hundreds of eyes staring at us; the least I could do was avoid unnecessary attention. It was warm out and still early morning. No doubt it would be another blistering hot day.

It didn't take long to find the school. It was a short twelve-minute drive up South Murphy Lane. The school was located just off Fourth East Street. It was partially made of maroon-colored brick and another section was a light brown. There was nothing special to it. Just a two-story building, a typical high school surrounded by trees and shrubs.

After parking out front, and getting a few odd looks from students who were huddled outside, I pulled my hood up, took a deep breath, pushed out of the vehicle and made a beeline for the entrance.

Inside, the sound of chatter filled the corridor. Several curious eyes looked our way as I scanned over the tops of people's heads searching for the office. Both of us headed for the main office to get directions. It didn't take long for them to give us our schedule and a map of the school before we went our separate ways.

"See you at lunch?" Zac asked.

"Maybe."

He got this concerned look on his face and shrugged. I adjusted the bag's strap on my shoulder and went in search of my first class. I tried to keep everything in perspective. One day of awkwardness that's all it was. Questions from students, advice from teachers and they'd be back to focusing on the drama that every school dealt with regularly. After finding the classroom, and taking a seat, I waited for all the other students. Slowly they streamed in and a few muttered to each other while glancing over. *Here we go.* Two kids gave a nod and took a seat across from me. One guy wearing a letterman jacket eyeballed me before heading to the back of the classroom and making a point to purposely scrape his chair out and slap his desk impatiently.

A dark-skinned kid slid into his desk beside me and leaned over.

"You don't want to sit there, that's Kyle's seat."

I got up and changed seats.

"I wouldn't sit there either," another guy said. "That's taken."

I ran a hand over my head and changed again.

"Nope. Not that one."

"You want to tell me where then?"

They cracked up laughing, just as the teacher came in.

"Alright settle down." He motioned with his hand for me to come up to the front. I eyed the others who looked to be finding the whole thing amusing. The teacher had a thick mustache and full head of hair, he sat down at his desk and pulled a handful of papers out of a brown leather binder. "You're Logan Matthews?"

"Yes sir."

He cast a glare out at the few others in the room. "You can take that seat over there."

He pointed to one chair I'd already sat in.

"But…"

"Matthews, they say it to anyone that's new. No one sits there."

I clenched my jaw and returned to my seat. Behind me I could hear chuckling. Yeah, this wasn't going well. I could feel eyes boring into me. *One year, that's it, and you are done,* I told myself.

Once the room filled up, I was grateful that the teacher didn't cause me any further embarrassment by introducing me, instead he pressed ahead with the lesson on art and design. Besides the odd passing comment as students handed in their work, the first class of the day went well, the ones that followed, not so, but that was to be expected. By the time lunch rolled around, I was ready to retreat into a corner and wait for Zac to show up. A familiar face would have been a godsend. When he did, there was another guy with him, and like anyone looking to fit in, he made a gesture to indicate he would sit with him. I didn't take offense. I gave a nod and continued eating lunch by myself for another ten minutes until they showed up.

They being two oddballs dressed in camouflage hunting gear, camo baseball caps, jacket and pants. They looked like they'd just walked out of the wilderness. All that was missing was a gun, or a bow.

"Can we mingle?" the tallest one asked, motioning to the empty seats.

I shrugged. It wasn't like they needed my permission.

His pal with straggly black hair and thick-rimmed glasses took a seat beside me, while the tall one with leather wristbands, a nose ring and wild frizzy hair tossed a brown bag in front of him and sniffed hard before speaking.

"I'm Bryce, though my friends call me Axl, and that's Scotty Moore."

I cast a sideways glance, and he saluted me with two fingers. "Just call me Bones."

I raised an eyebrow. "Right," I said slowly.

"And you are?"

"To be here? Lucky, I guess," I said in a sarcastic tone.

He chuckled and eyed Bones.

I continued. "Logan Matthews."

"So where you from, Logan?"

"South Dakota."

His eyebrows went up. "And you moved here?"

"Is that a bad thing?" I replied.

"That depends," he said turning his head and casting a gaze across the swath of students that were huddled into different cliques. Some stray ones threaded their way around outside wooden tables searching out a free seat. "You seen anything strange since you've been here?"

"Besides you two?"

He turned back and smiled.

Bones interjected, "You scoped out the Neanderthals?"

"The what?" I said nearly choking on my apple.

He sniffed again and pointed to a group dressed like bikers. "There's a class system here, Logan, the sooner you learn it, the sooner you survive. Of course if you pick the right one."

"Batter up!" Axl said, acting like he was hitting an

imaginary baseball and pointing it towards a bunch of biker-looking dudes. "First, we have the metalheads, the guys whose piss and shit hold their pants together, they have an aversion to deodorant, an addiction to leather, a taste for Metallica and Marlboro Lights, and ride nothing but Harleys, and scantily clad women."

He wiped his nose with the back of his arm. "Then, we have your run-of-the-mill geeks. Chess club champions, computer whiz kids, Dungeons & Dragons nerds. They get hard-ons over the latest Apple announcement, spend way too much time in textbooks, take everything literally and think conversation is a spelling bee. Yep, life is a time to shine, let's thank our parents for doing such a great job."

He bit down on his sandwich and squinted into the sun. "Then we have the stoners, barely noticeable, barely conscious, not much to say except they know a guy who can hook you up."

"Next we have your jocks. Stay out of their way because they have one year to make it all happen. You know, gain that parent-loving scholarship, work their way through the cheerleader squad and be crowned king at the next prom. Touchdown, bitches!"

Axl turned again, scrunching his nose up.

"Then we have what is more commonly found in Moab. Your little adventurers; hikers, bikers, climbers, rafters, horse riders, zip liners, oh gee dad, let's get together and save a tree. Yep, these nut huggers always see the glass half full, and even know a song about it. So crack out that rainbow strap guitar, share your feelings around the campfire and roast a few wieners on the weekends. And then… Well, Bones, would you like to do the honors?"

He gave a small bow. "My pleasure." He sucked in air between his teeth and his forehead wrinkled. "Last but not least, we have your nonconformist, aka, adrenaline junkies. BASE jumpers, skydiving heroes, slack liners, and the high-flying daredevils. Zero brains but who cares when you're a human glider. Yep, these dweebs are primo nut jobs."

Axl tapped me. "So there you go. Then there is all the rest. You, me, Bones. Us."

"Us?"

"The outsiders."

"And your point?"

"See anything unusual about these clusterfucks?"

I shrugged and made a face. "Nope."

"A little lopsided, don't you think?"

He could see I wasn't cluing in. "Until one week ago, the adrenaline junkies were a tight-knit group that comprised of four meatballs. Blake Davis, JT, Declan Knox and Zane Elliot. Surely you recognize them from their award-winning video of the meteor?"

I squinted at them. Sure enough it was them. Before I could reply he continued.

"Yep, they've been milking that shit for all it's worth. Now how many do you see over there?"

I craned my neck and Axl screwed up his face. "Don't stare, it's rude."

"Okay, if you say so." My eyes drifted over. I did a

quick head count. "Eighteen?"

Axl made a clucking sound with his tongue. "Exactly."

I shook my head and smiled. "You've lost me."

He clicked his fingers in front of my face and I backed up a little. I thought he would say something but instead he was indicating to Bones. Bones fished into his pocket and slipped across the table a business card. I picked it up.

PLANET ADVENTURE: Vacation Tours and Hunting Gear

"My old man runs it, drop by and we'll explain." He sniffed again and tapped his ear. "Too many freaks listening in." They got up to walk away. "Oh and hey, don't take too long thinking it over, Logan, it might be too late for you by then." I nodded and screwed up my face wondering what he meant by that.

Chapter 3

The last class of the day was history. Mrs. Palmer walked up and down the aisles between desks waving around a steel pointer as she detailed the history of Native American rock paintings, which depicted visions, clan symbols and recorded events. She had a full head of gray hair, beady eyes that looked over the rim of her glasses and a frail appearance.

Bones was in that class, every time I turned around he was staring at me and would give me this nod, as if he and I were privy to some greater understanding of the social class that dominated the school.

"There are many arguments about what these petroglyphs in Sego Canyon really mean. It's open to interpretation, however, what we know is that Anasazi and Fremont Native Americans dating back as far as 5000 B.C. created them. Some have interpreted them as nothing more than the ramblings of people under the influence of drugs, others tribal records and some have gone so far as to say they depict star people, an important moment in the timeline of human history. From China to Sumeria and throughout North and South America, similar drawings displayed beings with large craniums, eyes, physical size and incredible technology."

"I'm not saying it's aliens… but it's aliens," a voice muttered in the back and everyone cracked up laughing.

"Hilarious, Mr. Sanders, as you seem so knowledgeable on this topic, maybe you would care to explain what the serpent in this image refers to?" She wandered up the aisle and switched on an overhead projector. Then she asked one of the other kids to turn off the lights. There on the screen ahead were various symbols on a section of sandstone wall.

She flipped through them, one by one.

"It's referring to procreation. They were well hung."

She shook her head and put out the question to the class.

"Ms. Campbell?"

I turned my head towards a dark-haired beauty sitting a few seats back. I'd noticed her when I walked in. She was easy on the eyes and had a figure that would make anyone look twice.

She cleared her throat and looked as if she was daydreaming. "What?"

"The Sego petroglyph, Ms. Campbell. The serpent, what does it mean?"

"Sorry, history has never been my strong point."

"That's why you're here, Ms. Campbell. Now try again."

"The Anasazi were said to worship the sun, fire and serpents for fertility and agricultural productivity," I interjected.

Heads turned my way in the class.

Palmer got this surprised look on her face. "Fantastic, Mr...?"

"Matthews."

"Right. Anything else you wish to add?"

"They say star people bred with Native Americans to

create hybrid people."

"I told you, I wasn't that far off," Sanders said cracking a fist against a friend's hand. "It's all about probing."

That generated another wave of laughter before the bell rang loudly.

"Okay, I want you all to go over the material in the book and complete the assignment."

Students streamed out of the class and clogged up the corridor. Lockers banged, and chatter filled the air as everyone headed out for the day. Outside several yellow school buses were already filling up as I made my way over to the beat-up station wagon.

"Hey, fertility expert. I appreciate you jumping in back there. History…"

I cut in. "… not your strong point?"

"Biology, science is my preference." She smiled. "History not so."

"Nor mine, I just happened to do a little research on this place before coming."

The Sego Canyon was one of the many wonders

tourists were encouraged to visit on a trip through Moab. I'd just wanted to see what I was getting myself into before we arrived.

"That's right, how was your first day?"

I shrugged. "Weird."

We continued walking.

"Yeah, this place brings out the strange in people." She squinted into the late afternoon sun. "I'm Anna."

"Logan."

She nodded and adjusted her bag. "So what brought you out here?"

"Depends who you ask."

"I'm asking you."

My lip curled up. "A change. My mother used to live here. Her folks are from here. Perhaps you've heard the radio show... *Darker Perspective*?"

"That's..."

"Her father. My grandpa. Yep." I cringed.

She let out a laugh. "Like I said, this place brings out the strange in people." She ran a hand over her bubblegum lips. "So what about you? You believe all that mumbo jumbo he spouts?"

"No. But I should give you a forewarning. He's threatened to have us on his show."

"Huh! So you could be a big star by next week?" She chuckled.

I shook my head and snorted. "Not happening. It would be social suicide."

She motioned with her thumb to a motorbike a few cars down from our embarrassing excuse of a vehicle. "I'm over here. Take it easy, Logan." She walked a few steps, and I checked her out, she turned and smiled.

I felt a pat on my back at the exact moment he said, "Not a chance," in Zac's annoying voice. "She's way out of your league."

I wrapped my arm around his neck and brought him down to ruffle his head. I'd done it since he was old enough to talk back. We wandered back to the car and tossed our bags in the trunk before getting in.

"So how did you get on?"

"It was all right. It's not Dakota but I think the place might grow on me. You?"

I eyed Anna as she got on her bike and spoke to two friends.

"We'll see."

* * *

At home that evening mom had got us takeout. Apparently she hadn't had time to get to the grocery store in between touring homes with some real estate rep and trying to find a job. No one had any idea what gramps lived on but one glance inside his fridge provided clues. It was packed with bottles of beer, and the bottom shelf was filled with grapefruits.

"What's the deal with all the grapefruits?" I asked leaning on the open door and staring in amazement.

"He says it's good for his bowels."

"And the beer?"

"Logan, just come take a seat, have a bite and tell me how it went today."

Zac piped up. "So Mom, I got this invite to go to this

party tonight."

"Oh that's good, sweetheart. What home is it at?"

"It's not at a house, it's northeast of the town between Sand Flats Road and the river. They call the trail Hell's Revenge. A bunch of Jeeps are heading out there, and Elijah Davis is going."

"Who?" I said in unison with my mother.

"Elijah Davis."

"Any relation to Blake Davis?" I asked.

"Yeah, it's his brother."

Mom poured herself some water. "You know him, Logan?"

"Not exactly."

Our mom put her fork down and took a drink as I walked over. "Zac, I don't think that's a good idea. There will probably be a lot of drinking and you're only fifteen."

Zac groaned with a mouthful of food. "You said to make friends, and now I get an invitation and a chance to know people and you want to keep me at home?"

"I can take him," I said reaching for a plastic carton

filled with rice and chicken.

"I don't need a babysitter," Zac bellowed before puffing his chest out.

"How about we talk about this after dinner? How did it go for you today, Logan?"

I dug into my food, filling my mouth and hoping to avoid a long-winded conversation.

I shrugged. "It was okay."

"Make any friends?"

"Not really."

"You get to know any teachers?"

"Some."

The tension between us thickened as the questions persisted. She knew full well I was against the move from the beginning. She just wanted to hear that everything was great, and we were settling in. Anything that would reassure her that she'd made the right choice. She picked her fork back up and cocked her head to one side. "You could have stayed."

I shook my head. "Yeah well I didn't want to."

"I'm just saying."

I tossed my cutlery down, and it clattered causing both of them to look at me.

"It would have been easier, right? One less mouth to feed, one less person to deal with."

"Deal with?" She eyed me and pursed her lips. I knew right then I'd spoken out of turn. "Boy, you don't even know what I've had to deal with over the past year. Multiple trips to your school for fighting, visits from cops after they find you passed out drunk and…"

I pushed my food away and got up to walk away. I was sick of arguing. Ever since his death, we'd been at it. Twelve months of bickering back and forth. I knew she blamed me for his death.

"Where are you going?"

"Out."

"But what about taking me to the party?" Zac asked.

"Zac, you're not going!" I heard her yell as I slammed the door behind me.

Outside on the porch I exhaled hard. The dry air

wrapped around me like a blanket. I stared off into the night wishing I could take back what I said and just kept my mouth closed.

"Trouble in paradise?" gramps said. His voice startled me. He was barely visible. Nothing more than a dark silhouette off to the far side. He was resting in the porch rocker puffing away on his pipe. It glowed a hot orange. I cast a glance at him then stepped down off the porch and walked off into the night without saying a word.

Twenty minutes later, several miles away, I stood on the cusp of a rock looking out across the town, the lights of the homes lit up the night making it appear tranquil. I gazed down at the pocketknife in my hand and remembered the day he gave it.

"I want you to have this, kid, it belonged to my father, and his before him. I know we haven't seen eye to eye lately but I'm proud of you, son. No matter what you do once you graduate, I just want you to know I fully support you." I sighed and clutched it tight.

Chapter 4

Hobo trash can fires lit up the night. Music blared from Jeep speakers as a large crowd of teens danced beneath the stars in the Sand Flats Recreational Area. Blake Davis stood by the other four with a bottle of beer in hand and watched the fiasco play out before him.

Gathered on a landscape of petrified sand dunes and eroded remnants of ancient sea beds were twenty-four students, fourteen that were already changed, ten more than would make a new addition to the ever-increasing group that would eventually sweep across the land.

Five days, that's all it had taken to draw them in.

And many more would come.

They could speed up the process any time they liked by using the water source but this was the best part. He wanted to savor it this time. There was no rush. No need to end it quickly.

Others were out there, doing the same as him.

They were nothing more than specimens, like those before.

He eyed some of the new faces. Those that had been invited, those that he'd specifically requested to attend. One stood out to him — Malcolm Sanders.

He was a mouthy kid that didn't know when to keep it shut.

He'd heard the rumors.

The noise he'd made.

The way he showed disrespect.

Well, tonight would change all that.

Some were changed, others used as food. He already had in mind what he would do to him. His head leaned side to side. His eyes flickered, an oily blackness squeezing out what little white remained. One more race. One more planet.

"Blake," Elijah, his younger brother, said. "He didn't come. I'm sorry."

"It doesn't matter. There is plenty of time."

He looked up to the sky full of stars. It seemed almost

ironic that they were here.

"Well, guys? You ready?"

"Hell yeah."

They tossed their beers and one by one dropped off the huge sandstone rock, releasing their chutes and BASE jumping down into the party. It was one of many they would have over the coming days, weeks and months as they infiltrated the minds and lives of those around them.

Chapter 5

The next day at lunch it happened again. Though this time it was only Axl who showed up. He slumped down in front of me before I even saw him coming. He snagged one of my fries and tossed it into his mouth.

"Ain't this place just a freak show?"

He grinned as he cast his eyes around at the crowd of kids all divided into their cliques.

"I saw you talking with that little honey yesterday. So did you get her digits?"

"You stalking me?"

"People talk, especially about the new kid. Close observation, my friend. It helps to have eyes in the back of your head. Speaking of observation, notice anything different today?"

He eyed the adrenaline junkie group which appeared to have grown in number.

"So they've gained a few."

"And we've lost a few."

"What do you mean?"

He sniffed. "Walk with me."

"Look man, I'm just…"

"How's your kid brother?"

"What do you mean?"

He jumped up but not before snagging another fry and popping it into his mouth. I hesitated for a second before I got up and followed him, tossing the remainder of my lunch into a trash can.

"Hey!" I broke into a jog to catch up with him. Axl hurried out of the outside eating area, across a green field to the far side of a bike shed. There he pulled out a cigarette and lit one.

"Why did you mention my brother?"

"He didn't attend the party last night, did he?"

"How do you know about that?"

"Because I was there, so was Bones, keeping an eye on them." He twitched nervously and took a hard drag and blew it out while keeping an eye on a group of students.

"You were invited?" I asked.

"Not exactly but the Sand Flats Recreational Area is a vast piece of land, and my old man has some high-powered night vision binoculars that do wonders." He smiled and offered me a cigarette. I shook my head. Though I had my vices, smoking wasn't one of them. "I'm telling you, your kid brother was lucky he didn't show up. You need to keep a close eye on that one. Hanging out with Davis's brother and all."

"What the hell are you on about?"

He paused, just about to pull the cigarette away from his mouth. Smoke spiraled up, and he squinted. "You seen Malcolm Sanders today?"

"No."

"Notice any other desks empty?"

I shrugged. "A few. Why?"

I was getting a little tired of his vague questions.

"Let's just say that mouthy Sanders has opened his trap for the last time."

"You've lost me."

"He's in the ground, finito, gone… hasta la vista baby!"

Axl adjusted the strap on his shoulder.

"Filling his head with more of your conspiracy theories, spaceboy?" A female voice came from behind us. I turned to find Anna approaching with Bones. Bones was wearing a T-shirt that had the words I WANT TO BELIEVE on it.

He pulled a face. "They're not theories. We're talking facts. Real facts."

"So where's your proof? And please don't show poor Logan that grainy ass video. I've seen clearer Bigfoot videos online than that."

I screwed up my face. "What are you both talking about?"

Anna walked past me. "The odd couple here thinks that they're among us."

"Who?"

She gazed up and pointed. "Our star brothers." She hopped up onto a portion of wall that went around the bike area and leaned back to take in the warm sunshine.

"I didn't say that," Axl said stepping forward and jabbing his finger in her face. "You know full well that something strange is going on and after what me and Bones saw last night, there's no more doubt about it."

"Did they take you up to the mothership this time?"

"Really Anna, why do you have to be such a bitch?"

She flipped him the bird.

"We'll talk later, Logan," Axl said before tapping Bones on the chest and walking off leaving me alone with Anna.

I stared at them and looked back at her. "What was all that about?"

"Oh, his old man puts these crazy ass ideas in his head. I thought you would have known. His father helps your grandfather with that kooky radio show of his."

"That's his father?"

She smiled. "Yep!" She pulled out a bottle of orange soda from her bag, unscrewed the top and chugged it back. I remembered hearing my grandfather on the radio, and some other guy but never sat through an entire show to catch his name. I hopped up beside her.

"You hang out with those two?"

"God, no," she shot back before letting out a laugh. "Bones and Axl have been going around today warning people who've received an invite to the party to not go. They told me you were going tonight. Is that right?"

"I wasn't invited."

"Ah, you probably will be. There has been one every night for the past week."

"Is that normal?"

She squinted at me. "Nothing is normal around here. At Easter a whole whack of Jeeps drive around for nine days, the same thing happens on Memorial Day. Why? For the heck of it. Who the hell knows? So no, nothing is normal. Parties happen in the desert, usually on weekends, there is always one going on but just not as frequent as they have been."

"Who hosts them?"

"Blake Davis. Word gets around. Invites are spread.

People show up."

"And the cops don't do anything?"

"Oh they've tried. I'm guessing you didn't see that video of those three off-duty cops doing beer pong at some party a few months back? It went viral."

I chewed it over while looking at students milling around.

"What about those hanging out with Blake? You find that odd?"

"Do I need to answer that?"

"Right, everything's odd."

She put her drink back in her pack. "You're catching on. Anyway, you up for it tonight?"

I scratched the side of my face and looked off towards the school.

She must have caught my hesitation as she asked, "Please tell me you don't believe him?"

"Axl?"

She gave a nod.

I frowned. "No," I said then let out a laugh.

She hopped down off the wall. "Then pick me up around seven."

"I don't have a vehicle. I mean, a Jeep."

"So I'll swing by and pick you up."

"You don't have to do that."

"It's the least I can do after that little save you did yesterday."

"Oh I think she wouldn't have been that hard on you."

"You still have a lot to learn, Dakota."

"How do you know I'm from there?"

She smiled before turning away. "I asked around."

I couldn't help the smile that spread across my face.

"Hey, I didn't give you my home address."

"I already know it."

I chuckled. Anna broke into a jog and joined a group of girls before disappearing around a corner.

* * *

The bald-headed teacher scribbled furiously on the whiteboard while the rest of the class looked on. Some took notes, others were checking their phones. Bones was leaning across to Axl and they were discussing something and looking up at the board every few seconds. "So in summary, the Zika virus is transmitted to people primarily through the bite of an infected mosquito. Mosquitoes spread the virus during the day and night." He paused to take a breath before pressing on. "Now, we've already gone over the fact that while mosquitoes are often seen as a bloodsucking pest, it's not actually blood they need to survive, it's sugar. While both the female and male mosquitoes feed on nectar and plant juices for the sugar, it's the females that feed on blood in order to use the protein and iron found in blood to make their eggs. And of course we know that sugar — glucose, that is — is transported in the blood. And this sugar comes from the food we eat." He made a large period after it. "Can anyone tell me how this is done?"

A few kids mumbled, and the teacher didn't wait to get a clear answer.

"That's right, they use their mouthparts to pierce the skin of hosts and suck their blood while at the same time transferring their saliva into us to prevent the blood from clotting. In essence, mosquitoes — at least some of them — are like vampires. So now you might be asking why do some get bit more often than others?"

No one said a word or looked remotely interested.

"It's believed that they use a range of techniques to find their prey, some of which include the presence of carbon dioxide — the invisible, odorless gas we breathe out — and lactic acid, which is released through the pores of the skin, most commonly after exercise."

He scrawled a large line below it all and drew a crap picture of a mosquito.

"Finally, so we have a mosquito that has pierced your skin and begun sucking blood while injecting its anticoagulant saliva so that you don't know until you start to itch. Then this may or may not have a virus in it. They then use the protein and iron in the blood for their eggs. So where do they lay those?"

Once again silence dominated.

"Anywhere there is water," he continued.

Axl piped up asking a question, to which the rest of the class looked at him.

"Sir, how much water are we made up of?"

"That depends. If you are referring to the skin about 65%, the brain has 73%, the lungs 83%, the liver about 70%, the heart…"

"Okay, I think we get it," another student muttered, looking annoyed that Axl had said anything.

"So it's possible they could transfer these eggs to us?" Axl continued.

He laughed. "Mr. Ashburn, I see where you are going with this and yes, while some mosquitoes need water to hatch and yes, our bodies would make an interesting hatching ground, so to speak, it doesn't happen. Now of course that's not to say that parasites can't be passed from a mosquito to a human. There are more than 3,500 species of mosquitoes. Some of which are known to spread Zika virus, roundworm parasites and Dirofilaria immitis." He paused. "Heartworm."

"So they can carry parasites that could change us?"

"Um. Well, malaria is caused by a one-celled parasite called plasmodium and that has been passed on to humans through a mosquito bite. We experience change from having that in our system, and obviously not of the good kind."

Axl coughed and nudged Bones.

Bones interjected, "Sir, just an off-the-wall question. So, being as there are so many species that exist and you mentioned that mosquitoes feed on blood, transmit viruses and reproduce themselves in bodies of water... is it possible that if a species similar to the mosquito lived on another planet, it could feed on blood, transmit itself as a virus and repopulate or let's say duplicate themselves inside a host? One which was made up of mostly water?"

He chuckled. "It's plausible. You see, this is the beauty of what I'm trying to teach you in class. We are still finding species on our planet that defy what we know about feeding, breeding and reproduction."

The bells rang loudly.

"Okay everyone, see you tomorrow."

I tucked my books into my bag and was about to leave when Axl nudged me.

"Follow me."

He hurried out with Bones and I took a few more seconds to gather my things together.

Outside, they were lingering at the far end of the corridor. They waved me on looking anxious. I picked up the pace and made it to the end of the corridor and turned the corner only to find myself being grabbed and shoved into an empty classroom. Bones closed the door and dropped the blinds so no one could look in.

"Want to tell me what this is about?" I asked.

"Malcolm Sanders isn't the first one who has disappeared." Axl pulled out a moleskin notebook from his pocket and flipped it open. "Trish Wainright, Danny Norris, Rita Lopez, Aaron White, Brett Summers, Wendy Carter, James Harris... And the list goes on."

He tossed it down on one of the desks in front of me.

I shrugged. "So?"

"Every single one of them is missing. Gone. And you

know what all of them have in common?"

"I'm sure you're going to tell me."

"They showed up to the parties this past week."

I stared at the list. "So maybe they're off ill."

He laughed and looked at Bones who was peering out through the slats in the blinds.

"Show him the video," Bones muttered.

Axl nodded and pulled out his camera phone. He tapped the screen, swiped a few times and then handed it off to me. It was dark, grainy and besides seeing a few fires and the silhouette of people, I couldn't make out a damn thing.

I frowned starting to get annoyed by his weird behavior. "What am I looking at here?"

"Feeding, breeding and reproduction, my friend."

I lifted my head and met his gaze with a confused look. "You really are out of your mind." I tossed the cell phone back to him. "Anna was right about you two," I said as I headed for the door. "I'm outta here."

"It's happening, Logan, in this small town, right

underneath our noses. Now you can either wise up, or…"

I turned and pushed him back as he had a hold of my jacket.

"I don't know what you're smoking but let's just say for argument's sake, that you were right. Why—"

"I am," he said cutting me off.

I narrowed my gaze. "Why wouldn't the parents of these kids be kicking up a fuss? This would be all over local and national news."

"Because they're selective."

"Selective?"

"Yeah, they know the ones that aren't going to be missed and those that will. One makes a tasty snack, the other is changed and joins the ever-growing group of neophytes that grace us with their presence each day."

I let out a laugh. "Is that so?"

"I'm telling the truth, Logan."

"Bullshit. You're playing mind games."

I stared at him waiting for his next clever answer.

"Look, you want to know why no one has said

anything? Do you know who Blake's father is?"

"Who?"

"The chief of police."

"And?"

He blew his cheeks out. "Get with the program, Logan. They have already infiltrated the cops, the school and most likely the parents."

I stared at him unable to believe that he had come up with this cockamamie theory. It wasn't just ridiculous, it was batshit crazy and the last thing I needed to be dealing with. I already had enough on my plate. I pointed my finger at him, then Bones. "You are out of your damn minds."

I pushed past him and made a motion for Bones to get out of the way.

"Tonight, Logan. See for yourself. But don't say I didn't warn you."

Chapter 6

I'd just stepped out of the shower and was in the middle of getting ready to head out when my mother knocked on the door.

"Logan, you decent?"

"Give me a second."

I slipped on a pair of jeans and a shirt.

"Come in."

She entered and looked around. "You know, this used to be my room when I was a kid."

"Really?"

She smiled and nodded. "Listen, I need you to keep an eye on Zac tonight, I have an opportunity to shadow a dispatcher down at the police department."

I smiled. "They hired you?"

"Why does that surprise you? I've done the work before. I'm more than qualified. They want me to see how they operate and get to know their system."

I shifted my weight from one foot to the next. "But I thought you weren't looking to do that anymore?"

She stared back at me in disbelief.

"When we were in Dakota. Now we need the money, Logan, and I have had no word back from the other places in town."

"But it's only been a couple of days."

"And so it's a good thing I've landed this." She frowned. "I would have thought you would have been pleased. The sooner I can bring money in, the sooner we can get a place of our own." She shook her head. "What is up with you, Logan? And all this attitude lately you've been giving me is taking its toll."

I pointed towards the door. "Can't gramps look after him? I was just getting ready to head out for the evening."

"Where?"

"To a party."

"Alcohol?"

"Of course not, I'm not twenty-one."

"That hasn't stopped you before."

I blew out my cheeks and looked at my wristwatch. Anna would be here soon.

"I have someone coming to pick me up, so can we do this another time?"

"I'm sorry, Logan, you will have to contact whoever it is and tell them you can't come. Grandpa is out tonight. He is meeting up with a friend for drinks."

I ran a hand through my hair. "You've got to be kidding me?"

She shifted her weight from one foot to the next and glared at me. "Logan, I rarely ask you for anything, I need you to do this for me."

"Rarely? No, you never ask, you just tell us."

"That's not fair," she shot back.

"Like it was fair to not ask us about moving out here?"

We eyed each other, and she looked as if she was about to blow her top but instead she turned and headed out. "Just do it, Logan."

With that said she slammed the door, and I stood in the silence gritting my teeth. I couldn't even phone Anna as I didn't have her number, so she would show up and then I'd look like a complete fool. I slumped down on my bed and gazed up at the ceiling. Outside the door I could hear mother getting ready, keys jangling, the clatter of heels and telling Zac that I would look after him. Of course, he protested.

"There are some frozen meals in the fridge you can nuke in the microwave. Don't wait up, I'll probably be back later tonight."

I reached over and grabbed up a Hacky Sack off a side table and tossed it around in my hands, then flicked on the small TV in the corner of the room. I surfed through the channels a few times until stopping on a news broadcast that was issuing a warning alert about a solar storm across the bottom of the screen. I began reading it when the door burst open and in charged Zac whining about the microwave dinners being low-calorie diet food that tasted like crap.

"You think we can walk down to the pizza shop in town?"

I frowned. "Quiet, I'm trying to hear this."

I swung my legs off the bed and turned up the volume.

"Bigger and more immediate than the threat of a hurricane they say is the threat of a solar storm. What most don't know but has only now been made official is that earth's magnetic field, which acts as our protective shield in space, has a hole in it. And that can place all of us at risk. I have with me today, Doctor Hale Lewis, professor and author of the book 'In the Eye of the Storm' to discuss this. Welcome, good evening and how are you?"

The screen split and a beady-looking fella with flyaway hair and spectacles stared back.

"I appreciate you having me."

"Okay, so let's get straight to it. What is this solar shield, how much danger are we in and should we be making preparations now?"

He breathed in. *"Okay, so the sun every eleven years releases a shockwave, a tsunami of radiation that could wipe out our communications, weather satellites, GPS, internet, cell phones and much more."*

"Hold on a minute. So you are saying my iPhone would stop working?"

"Like I said, cell phones, internet, TV, cable, satellites, planes, vehicles that operate using computer chips could be wiped out. Essentially when we have the peak of the sunspot cycle, it can destroy susceptible electronic equipment over a wide area and even shutting down the entire power grid."

"How?"

"Well the sun's magnetic field flips. The north and south pole flip and release a shockwave of radiation that would hit the earth and wipe out a large chunk of our satellite communications."

"And how quickly can that happen?"

"Solar flares can occur within minutes. A CME is slower, and most commonly known to take anywhere from one to three days to hit earth, but that's all based on the speed and whether it slows down along the way. No two CME events are ever the same. A CME traveling at 1000 km/s could take only one day; another traveling at 400 km/s could take five days. But again that's just a rough guide, it could arrive *earlier or later than what we predict. And realistically, we really don't know the power of that CME until it hits. We got lucky with the Quebec blackout in 1989, it could have been far worse."*

The interviewer took a deep breath. "Okay but you are saying this only happens every eleven years?"

"Yes and no. Small ones occur often, like the ones in 2003 and 2005. There was only a two-year difference there. And we narrowly missed a huge one in 2012. So most have assumed we won't have another one until around 2023, however, with the solar flares over the past week and the meteors hitting earth, there is a very strong possibility we could be on our way to seeing a solar storm within a matter of hours."

The interviewer screwed up his face. "Hold on a second. Hours? But you said a day, or five days?"

"Yes, and that's why there have been news alerts released by the Space Weather Prediction Center over the past five days about a potential solar storm."

"Okay, you are scaring me, doctor. So let's get back to the

cycle. Why eleven years?"

Right then Zac stood in front of the TV.

"Come on, Logan, I'm getting hungry."

I shoved him to one side. "Get out of the way. I'm trying to hear this."

"It takes eleven years for the magnetic field of the sun to build up enough intensity to go through the process of doing that flip. It occurs in the center and like the inside of a clock that is wound up, once it's wound up a little too tight, it springs out of control. All of this means we have to think about how we can reinforce our satellites, building redundant systems—"

"Redundant?"

"It's a term used in engineering. It refers to the duplication of a component or functionality of a system intending to increase its reliability in the form of a backup or fail-safe. Improving the system could help prevent GPS, the power grid and all forms of satellites used for communication from being disrupted."

"So there is nothing to be done in space but we can do

things here?"

"If we had enough time."

"Had? Do we have backup systems in place, doctor?"

"I can't speak for what the government or companies have or don't have in place. I'm just saying we need to look at this. However, we might be too late. You see as scientists we made a mistake."

"A mistake?"

"We thought the next cycle wouldn't happen until 2023. Well some of our data was off and that's why we are issuing the alert now. The next cycle that appears to be peaking could be much more serious than we thought."

"I'm confused here, doctor, are you saying we will get a solar storm for sure?"

"I'm saying in the past we have dodged the bullet, we have more satellites up there now than ever before, we have this hole in the earth's magnetic field, and as much as we like to think we are ready — we aren't. Unfortunately earth is not prepared for an event like what was seen in 1859 and based on the raw data that has come in, it's possible we could

experience a mass blackout before the day is out."

"Mass blackout? Of the USA or the world?"

"That is to be seen. Though viewers would be advised to make preparations."

The interviewer chuckled nervously as the image on the screen crackled a little. "Doing what?"

The doctor turned to someone off the screen and looked concerned.

"I'm going to have to leave, I'm sorry."

"Doctor, please, just a few ideas would help our viewers."

He sighed and glanced off to his left, he muttered something then looked back at the camera. "Unplug electronics, shield important devices and create a poor-man's faraday cage out of aluminum foil or Mylar for protecting things like a two-way handheld battery-powered radio, CB radio, portable shortwave battery-powered SW/AM radio, LED flashlights, solar battery chargers, and oh and if need be, bury sensitive equipment. Not much will work after a CME but some of those devices will and the rest, well if the grid goes down it could take a long time to recover, and we may never recover. That's it for now. I've got to go."

"Logan!" Zac bellowed.

"What?" I yelled in frustration trying to focus on what he was saying.

Zac hit the power button, and the TV winked out.

"Earth to Logan. Forget solar storms. We have a food crisis right now. I'm starving, grandpa is out and mom said you would look after me."

"For goodness' sakes, you don't need looking after."

He leaned against the doorway.

"I know that. You know that. But tell that to my stomach, and…"

I threw my hands up. "All right. All right. But there's a problem."

"What?"

"I have to go out tonight."

"But mom said…"

"No buts, I told Anna I would go with her."

"Anna? The dark-haired hottie? No way. You did not score a date with her."

I tossed the Hacky Sack at him and bounced off the bed and continued getting ready. I tore off the loose shirt and threw on a white T-shirt.

"If I get you some pizza, you need to promise to not tell mom I went out."

He got this mischievous grin on his face. "Where are you going?"

"To a party."

"Where?"

"Sand Flats."

His mouth widened. "Oh come on. I was invited yesterday, and I never got to go."

"Too bad," I replied as I slipped on a pair of sneakers before scrambling around for my damn wallet.

"Take me with you then."

"No. That is completely out of the question."

"And so is going out when mom told you specifically—"

I grabbed a hold of him by the collar.

"You hit me, I call mom."

I narrowed my eyes, clenched my jaw and released him. Right then headlights washed across the window and I pushed back the thin drapes.

It was Anna.

"Oh crap." I turned my attention back to Zac. "Bro, I can't take you. There is going to be a lot of drinking going on, and there are few things I need to..."

Zac pulled his cell phone out from his back pocket.

"Who are you dialing?"

"Mom."

I snatched the phone out of his hand and he bolted out of the door heading for the landline in the kitchen. He was within arm's reach when I scooped him up in a tackle and we piled into the table and chairs. The remains of Zach's uneaten dinner flew in the air, along with several glasses of water. We crashed hard just as the doorbell rang.

Both of us froze.

I shot Zac an annoyed glance. His eyes lit up. "Okay, you can come but you are to stay near me at all times, no going off and no drinking, smoking or telling Anna about… well… anything."

He gave a wry smile. "Deal. You go get changed as you have microwave pizza on you and I'll go answer the door." Zac scrambled to his feet before rushing off. I darted out of the kitchen back into my bedroom and tore off the tomato sauce-stained shirt and tossed on a purple Minnesota Vikings T-shirt. From beyond the door I could hear Zac inviting Anna in.

I splashed on cologne, ran fingers through my dark hair and checked my teeth.

All good.

I coughed into my hand and did a quick breath test.

That's when I felt it. I was in such a rush to get changed that I hadn't noticed my jeans had a wet patch right near the groin. The water must have splashed over it when we fell. I could now feel it soaking through.

"Yeah, he's just in his room. Come this way."

My eyes widened in horror. The room was a complete state. Clothes strewn across the floor, a hamper basket turned on its side. Textbooks open on the table, a pair of underpants hanging over the side table and several of gramps's old Playboy magazines open on the bed. Frantically, I grabbed at different items as I heard the sound of feet coming down the hallway. I stuffed it all into a closet that was already filled with grandpa's crap, then shot across the room and peeled off my jeans. I was trying to squeeze into the next pair just as the door creaked open.

I had one leg in and the other partially there when I lost my balance and toppled to the floor. There, I found myself looking up at an amused Anna.

"Need a little help?" Zac asked, his face breaking into a big grin.

Chapter 7

We could see the glow of fires illuminating the party, long before we arrived.

I was riding shotgun in the front with Anna. She drove like a maniac down the back streets of Moab until we made it beyond the lights of the town, then cut through the darkness of the desert. The air was thick with dust. Temperatures were hovering in the high seventies. Her Jeep Wrangler bounced over rough terrain as we made the short ten-minute trip out to the Sand Flats Recreation Area.

"Hey, I'm really sorry about having to bring my brother along."

She shrugged. "That's okay, I had a sister a few years younger than him."

"Had?"

There was a moment of hesitation before she replied. "She passed away from cancer."

"Shit. I'm sorry to hear that."

She nodded. Now I felt like an idiot.

"You do know I can hear you both?"

I twisted around and eyeballed him. That was all that was required to get him to shut it. He was squished between two of Anna's friends. A guy and a girl who were in the same year as me. For someone that had lost a family member, she didn't show any signs of struggle, then again I'd also tried to keep the past under wraps. It was easier that way. Fewer questions made for less awkward moments.

"So you always lived in Moab?" I asked.

"Born and raised."

"Your parents? What do they do?"

Wind whipped through our hair as there was no top on the Jeep.

"My mother is a doctor at the hospital, my father works as a ranger at Arches National Park. And yours?"

I hesitated before replying. "Actually my mother just landed a job as a dispatcher with Moab Police."

"Oh, neat. Did she do that before?"

I nodded but didn't go into details about our father, hoping she might shift the topic — she didn't.

"And your father?"

I cleared my throat. "He's no longer with us."

"Oh, he bailed on you, did he?"

"Dead actually."

Only the roar of the engine and the distant sound of music could be heard.

"Sorry."

Zac leaned forward, his head coming into view like a turtle extending its neck to peer beyond the shell. "Died in a car crash, isn't that right, Logan?"

I shot him a glance. It had been one subject that was rarely raised. Not because it was too painful to talk about though that factored into it. It was because of how the accident happened. Anna must have seen that the topic bothered me so she changed the topic.

"What are you going to do after graduation?"

"College, I guess."

"Right, but do you have in mind what you want to do?"

"Do you?" I shot back.

Her guy friend, Adam, in the back piped up. "Anna here wants to be a skydiving instructor, ain't that right?"

I looked at both of them. "Is that right?"

"No." She laughed. "I have other things I would prefer to do."

"Like biology?" Adam said cracking up laughing. "Oh yeah that's real exciting."

"It might save your life someday," Anna shot back. She turned back. "You ever done it?"

"Skydive? No."

"You should. It's one hell of a rush."

"Is that why you wanted to come out tonight? Because of Blake and the others?"

She shook her head. "No."

"Yes it was, don't lie," Olivia, her friend in the back, said.

She laughed. "Okay, my curiosity was piqued. They've

always been this tight-knit group that for the longest of time kept people at a distance."

"But what's the big deal?"

"Big deal?" Adam asked before leaning forward and producing his cell phone. "Let's give Logan here a quick course in what these lunatics do for fun." He brought up an online video and turned it around and hit play. It showed someone filming three guys soaring forward off a cliff while getting dangerously close to cliffs and trees. They were performing all manner of stunts and tricks while yelling like complete idiots.

"It's called low terrain flying. You get a lot of folks who do wingsuit jumps but they don't risk going that low and doing stunts. That's just one of the many crazy things these guys do. They've made a name for themselves online and rumor has it, even landed a sponsorship with Red Bull."

"Yeah, many companies send them free shit to film themselves pushing the envelope," Olivia added.

"Do they have a death wish?" I asked.

"Seems so."

Adam leaned back. "Anyway that's just one of the many off-the-wall things they do in their spare time."

"And they haven't injured themselves?"

"Not yet. But the way I see it, it's only a matter of time."

There was silence as I chewed it over.

"So why have they started throwing these parties?"

Anna shrugged. "No idea, most people just go to watch them do crazy stuff. It's pure entertainment."

As we got closer to the entrance of the recreational area, the boom of bass music got louder. There was a line of Jeeps parked on either side, and a muscle-bound guy taking tickets before he would let people in.

Anna eased off the gas as the guy approached. He was draped in glow stick necklaces and bracelets, and covered in green and purple neon paint.

"Tickets."

Anna handed them over and he shone a light across everyone's faces.

"Four tickets, five people. You need another ticket."

I leaned across. "It's my kid brother, I'm just keeping an eye on him."

"No can do. No ticket. No entry."

"Come on, man, give us a break this one time."

"Not my rules."

A few Jeeps behind us honked their horns as we were holding everyone up.

"I guess none of us are going in then," Anna said jamming the gearstick into reverse so she could back out.

"Look, hold up." The guy glanced off to his side. "All right you can go in, just don't tell anyone."

"You're a sweetheart," Anna said reaching across and stroking under his chin before tearing away. The others in the back let out a laugh. We followed the line of Jeeps rolling over the sand flats. It was like an army of ants. Headlights washed over the red terrain and it felt like we were on the surface of Mars. It was a colorful display of lights, fire and neon colors as a large crowd gathered a few minutes away. Sparks from hobo trash cans hovered up into the night sky. Vehicles were everywhere. Music boomed loudly. Between the stars in the sky and neon glow lights, it was clear to see the attraction.

"Cool, huh?" Anna said as she parked and hopped out.

"I've never been to anything like it."

The music got louder the closer we got to the others. We elbowed our way through an ocean of familiar faces. I turned to Zac who looked wide-eyed. *Oh man, mom will kill me if she gets home early.* That's all I could think about.

"Zac, stay close," I yelled, but the music smothered my words.

We made it into the heart of where it was all happening. There were six or seven tables set up with kegs, and even more cases of beer below. Four people were taking money and handing out drinks while some were offering people LSD. The smell of marijuana dominated the air, and everyone appeared to be having a good time.

I felt someone tug at my back and turned to see Zac

with another kid, the same one from school. He thumbed over his shoulder. "I'm gonna be just over there, okay?"

I pointed at him and yelled into his ear. "Don't go off. Stay close."

He waved me off. "Settle down, I'm not a kid."

I rolled my eyes. He disappeared into the crowd and soon was lost in the darkness.

"Come on," Anna said grabbing up a couple of beers and handing me one. She began to sway in time with the music. Though I wanted to loosen up, I couldn't help feel distracted by the memory of Axl's grainy video. It was hard to tell what I saw, but something wasn't right. I tried to relax and push it out of my mind. This was what it was all about — a new town, new friends, and a beautiful girl.

It didn't take long before the buzz of the alcohol kicked in, and I felt my inhibitions melt away. The music bellowed, and the lights blurred. I could see Anna before me, then lights, and then dark eyes. What the heck? I shook my head and looked again and everything was normal.

I'm not sure how many hours we danced for before I felt nauseated. It was hard to tell if it was the alcohol or just the heat of the day finally taking its toll.

"You okay?" Anna spoke loudly into my ear. I caught the aroma of her perfume — it was intoxicating.

I threw up a hand. "I'm fine, I need…" I pulled at my T-shirt. "I just need to get a drink of water." She nodded and continued to dance with Adam and Olivia. The drone of the bass was giving me a headache. There was a line of blue porta-potties off in the distance. I made a beeline for them, and got inside one. I braced myself using both hands and felt myself lurch and toss up what I'd just had. I figured it must have been what I'd eaten earlier in the day or just a touch of heatstroke. I wiped the side of my mouth and leaned back, just taking a few seconds before heading out.

As I was standing there, I heard what sounded like two people enter the one stall beside me. I could hear a girl giggling and a guy telling her how gorgeous she was and that he'd always wanted to do it in a porta-potty. Even in my hazy state, I shook my head. This was the last place I would have wanted to get it on. It stunk to high heaven.

When I no longer felt as if I would hurl, I was just about to leave when I heard someone gasping next door. Hands battered the sides of the plastic, and I shook my head. Someone was getting lucky.

My hand turned the dial to unlock the door when they croaked out.

"What are you doing? Stop!" a male voice said.

I frowned.

Now I'd been on many a camping trip in the past and heard people getting it on. Sure, some were wild and noisy as hell but that didn't sound like someone enjoying themselves.

I listened intently, thinking maybe my mind was playing tricks on me. By the way I was feeling I had begun to think that someone had roofied my drink.

There were no more words heard, just a muffled sound. Then it was over.

I heard a door unlock, and I quickly unlocked mine. I

saw some girl walking off and the door she'd come out of, slightly ajar. I was just about to reach for the door and take a look inside when a hand clamped down on my shoulder. Startled I spun around.

"Whoa!" Anna threw up her hands. "There you are. I was looking for you over at the tables. You feeling okay?"

I looked back into the porta-potty and shook my head.

"Yeah, I think maybe I had a little too much to drink."

"Come on, there's a bunch of kids doing stunts on bikes. They're all lit up in LED lights. You got to see this."

As we broke into a jog, I glanced back one final time unsure of what I heard. We hurried across the dunes, scrambled up to an outcropping of rock and looked out across heads bouncing to the rhythm of music. There had to have been at least two hundred people, perhaps even more.

"Is there usually this many?" I asked.

"Never been," she replied.

Suddenly there was a roar of engines and four dirt

bikes came tearing over a high plain of slickrock domes. One of them did a backflip and landed, another one went over the top of him as two more crisscrossed. All of them were lit up in neon, and releasing a trail of orange smoke from the back like the way stunt planes did, except this was full of golden sparks.

"Can I ask a personal question?" Anna asked as I stared at the outrageous stunts they were performing. Each one was better than the last. It was a tantalizing displaying of skill and color.

"Sure."

"You went quiet when I asked about your father. Do you mind me asking what happened?"

I cast a glance at her before focusing on the rest of the crowd.

"My father was a cop." I picked up a small stone and rolled it around in my hand. "I was out at a party and had a lot to drink. We all did. Anyway, I passed out and a friend of mine gave me a lift home. That friend had been drinking as well that night and on the way back, a cop tried to pull him over." I tossed the stone out and gave a strained smile. "Seems my friend thought he could outrun him. He did but not before causing the officer to crash. That cop was my father." I paused. "I was in the back, oblivious to it all. When the cops finally got him to stop, the next thing I remember was waking up in a car that had been ditched and having my wrists cuffed."

I reflected upon the event. All the emotions welled up; the trip to the hospital, my mother breaking down and the look of pure shock on Zac's face.

"My father didn't make it."

She didn't respond.

"Yeah, quite the buzz killer, isn't it?"

"That's rough."

I picked out another stone and stared at it in my hand before tossing it.

"Though she hasn't said it. I know my mother blames me."

"No, you can't think that way. You weren't driving, Logan."

"I know, I wasn't the one driving, hell, I wasn't even aware of it all happening but that doesn't matter. I was in the car that caused the accident, I'm here and he's gone."

"Still," Anna said. "I'm sorry you had to go through that."

"Yeah, so am I." I exhaled hard and glanced at my watch. "I should get my brother home. It's getting late."

"Right, I'll go track down Adam and Olivia. The last I saw them, they were smoking weed with a group nearby." She let out a gentle chuckle and Anna hurried down, disappearing into the crowd. I stood up and wiped dust off my jeans before narrowing my gaze and trying to spot Zac. A task that wasn't easy being as there were so many people. As I made my way down and squeezed through the crowd, I felt a hand on my shoulder.

"Logan Matthews."

I turned to find Blake Davis smiling. He was dressed in dirt bike gear.

He gave a nod to the crowd. "How you liking it?"

"Impressive," I said.

"Ah, you should have seen us in the canyons on Memorial Day. We used old bikes, a ramp, and then parachuted down."

I made a face like I was impressed and continued to scan faces for my brother.

"Come have a drink with us."

"Actually, I'm…"

He wrapped an arm around my neck and pulled me away from the others.

"Well I guess one more drink would be okay."

Blake led me up a steep sandstone dome to meet the rest of his buddies who were standing beside their bikes whacking back bottles of beer and talking among themselves.

"JT, Declan, Zane… meet Logan Matthews."

One of them clasped my hand while the other two gave a nod. Blake hunched over and pulled out a bottle of beer from a cooler and handed it to me.

"So how you liking Moab, Logan?"

I shrugged. "It's okay I guess."

He glanced at my T-shirt.

"You a big Vikings fan?"

"Most are in Dakota, that or Packers."

"Never been one for sports, at least not unless it's the extreme kind. Hey, guys!" he said as JT gave him a high-five.

I twisted the top of the bottle and knocked it back.

"So you ever BASE jump?"

"No but I ride."

"Well look at that, Matthews rides. There's hope for you yet."

They all cracked up laughing as if they were privy to some inside joke. His laughter slowly dwindled until he got this dead serious look on his face. "Must be hard being new to the town and all, fitting in and whatnot? We know a thing or two about that, don't we, guys?"

They nodded with wicked grins on their faces.

I shrugged. "It's going okay, I guess."

"But it could always be better, ain't that right, boys?"

They each nodded, eyeing me with a sly expression.

Blake walked up to an edge on a portion of the rock and looked down on the crowd. As I watched him, I kept an eye on the other three. As crazy as it seemed, I couldn't help think about what Axl and Bones had said about them. They seemed ordinary enough — that was until what came next.

"Fitting in, it's all about making the right choices." He chuckled and wrapped his arm around me and walked me over to the edge. "Tell me, Logan, did you see anything catch your eye?"

I screwed up my face. "What?"

He pointed down towards the ground and singled out one in the crowd.

"The girl. The one you spotted coming out of the latrine. Did you see anything?"

I shook my head. "I'm not sure what you mean?"

He smiled then released me. "Well boys, let's show Logan here what we mean, shall we?"

"Hell yeah!" they roared.

Chapter 8

What should have been a night of fun quickly turned into terror. Blake and the other three hopped on to their bikes and brought them to life with a deafening roar. His lip curled at the corner as the back wheel tore up the sandstone and they shot away at a high rate of speed, heading straight for the crowd. *What the heck?*

My eyes widened and jaw dropped as each of them hopped up on to their seats as if they were about to stand. The guttural roar of their engines was lost in the volume of music, pounding out electronic beats. A few students on the outer perimeter turned and tried to react but it was too late, the heavy-duty dirt bikes plowed into them. Blake, JT, Declan and Zane launched themselves in the air as if they were performing a stage dive at a concert — except this was no concert.

It happened so fast. One second people were dancing, oblivious to anything except the beat, and the next they were scrambling to escape from the beasts among them.

Blake landed hard on top of a guy twice his size, then disappeared beneath an ocean of bodies. The other three did the same. When Blake came up the lower half of his face was covered in blood. He gazed back, a smile flickered before he clamped hold of a young girl by the throat and then...

I staggered back unable to believe what I seeing.

It was like watching a train wreck. I couldn't pull my eyes away.

Like a viper snake attacking its prey, he lunged forward, head jerking backwards as a long tubular mouthpart shot out past his lips and pierced the side of her throat. Her mouth widened in horror. She flailed in desperation but it did little to help — then, as if drained of blood, her face sank in and he released her. The body collapsed to the dusty ground, nothing more than shriveled skin and bone.

The revolting tubular mouthpart shot back in, and he wiped his lips with the back of his hand while eyeing me with a devilish grin.

The screams of those nearby were lost in the drug and alcohol fueled haze and the heavy pounding of music. Those that tried to flee were tackled to the ground and picked off by others in the crowd just like Blake.

Like a vicious animal attack that showed no mercy, they turned on unsuspecting prey.

"Holy shit," I muttered, backing up. Terror, confusion and fear mixed to create a chemical cocktail that almost paralyzed me. My mind struggled to comprehend what I was seeing. Was this some kind of hallucination? I dropped the bottle of beer in my hand. The glass shattered and the golden liquid trickled away.

The terrifying attacks continued.

Down below it was pure pandemonium.

Some were unaware of what was happening around them.

The four teens, along with others from their group, turned on the rest, attacking from every angle without hesitation. My eyes scanned the faces. Adam, Olivia,

Anna.

Zac!

Not wasting another second, I bolted down with little thought to my safety. I gave the crowd a wide berth, then shouldered my way through like an NFL player hoping to score a touchdown. Drinks flew in the air as I knocked multiple people to the ground, driven by panic.

Anna was the first one I spotted. I fixed my eyes on her and barreled through, not slowing for even a split second. As I collided with her, a cup of beer went all over her top.

"Logan, what the hell?"

Not even replying, I grabbed her by the wrist, hauling her up and practically dragging her on through a mob of dancers. "Move it. Run."

She resisted, yanking her arm free.

"Get off. Are you on drugs?"

I barely heard what she said as my eyes homed in on the savagery occurring just beyond a line of kids. It was like being stuck in the middle of a cornfield having a combine harvester bearing down on me. One after the next, bodies dropped like cornstalks.

"You want to live, run!"

Finally she followed my gaze and saw what I was staring at. Her jaw dropped as Olivia and Adam were taken down. I gripped her hand and plowed through the mass of bodies, hurdling over the fallen as we made a mad dash in the direction I'd last seen Zac. Dozens scrambled for their vehicles, screaming as the realization of danger sank in.

But this wasn't their first crack at the whip.

Many were taken down before they could even break the perimeter of the crowd.

It was hard to tell which way to go. It wasn't like they had the face of a monster. That was what was so terrifying. Unless we witnessed an attack, or saw blood dripping from their jaw, there was no way of knowing who was one of them.

Just when I thought it couldn't get any worse, it did. As Jeeps roared to life, and death spread across the crowd, suddenly all the power cut out. One second music was booming, headlights washed over us, the next the landscape was smothered in darkness.

All that could be heard were the cries of those trying to flee.

"No, no, no!" I yelled as my eye scanned the crowd. Without power and lights, I couldn't see where Zac was. All I heard were the final cries of those succumbing to the vicious attacks.

"Zac!" I shouted, but it was pointless.

"Logan, we have to go."

"No. My brother…"

She screamed my name. "Logan!"

The desert at night was beyond dark, the only illumination came from the stars and after the blinding lights shut off, my eyes were still trying to adjust. Anna pulled at my hand, tugging me towards the silhouette of vehicles. Seconds seemed like minutes. When we dived into her Jeep, she put her key in the ignition and tried to start the engine but it wouldn't start. In that moment I knew. Streaking across the sky, there was an array of swirling colors. The Northern Lights. *This can't be happening. Not here. Not now.*

The confusion was so overwhelming, my mind couldn't handle it.

"I've got to find my brother."

I hopped out of the vehicle.

"Logan, no."

Right then as I turned, a body landed on me, knocking me to the ground. It was a female, her head flipped back, her mouth opened and a foul-looking, snake-like mouthpart shot out of her mouth. Forcing her back, trying to get her off me, I turned my face away from the sight of the slippery stinger.

Then, in that instant before it pierced my skin, the girl fell to one side and Anna appeared looming over me with a tire iron in her hand. She'd just nailed that bitch in the head.

She grabbed my hand, and I knew right then any hope of finding Zac was lost. There were too many. Nothing but screams and chaos dominated the night.

"We have got to go."

She didn't need to convince me. We burst forward, sprinting away from the vehicles with a dozen others. Tortured cries filled the darkness as one by one people were taken down and either consumed or turned into one of them. What were they? How soon did people change? This was unlike anything I could imagine. Adrenaline shot through me pumping my legs like pistons.

Behind more of them came rushing after us like a pride of lions hunting us.

I thought this was it. That it was all over.

Seconds from now I would feel one latch on to my back, then...

I squinted into the distance.

Like a speck on the horizon, I saw it. At first I thought it was a figment of my imagination, another hallucination like seeing an oasis in the middle of the desert. The light bounced a few times, and then the roar of the engine reached my ears.

It was a truck.

What followed next was gunfire, multiple rounds.

It was like being in a fucking war zone. I didn't know whether to zig or zag as the surrounding sandstone was torn up. Like a freight train heading directly at us, the light got brighter and bigger until seconds from collision it swerved.

"Get in!" a familiar voice bellowed as hands hauled us up into the back of a truck and more gunfire erupted.

"Get us out of here, Bones."

Tires squealed, and rounds deafened us as we tore away into the night leaving behind a bloody massacre. As the truck bumped its way over potholes, and the terrain changed from a dusty road to regular asphalt, only one thing dominated my mind — Zac.

Chapter 9

It was late; I was exhausted but sleep was the last thing on my mind. "My brother is back there."

"I'm sorry, man, but we are not going back." Axl pulled me up from the bed of the vehicle and that's when I realized what I was in. It was my grandpa's truck.

"How did you get this?"

"We borrowed it, kid. Don't worry, your grandpa gave the green light," a familiar voice muttered from up front. The man turned around, and I squinted. It looked like he'd been to a costume party and had dressed up like Indiana Jones.

"Logan, meet my father."

"Vern Ashburn, pleased to make your acquaintance. Your grandpa has told me a lot about you." He extended a callused hand between the seats while the other held on to an AR-15. I shook his hand and stared at him a little apprehensive.

"You want to tell me how this truck is working?"

Vern shot back. "Better question, why the hell were you out there?"

"It was a party," Anna said.

"I tried to tell them, Dad," Axl said. "Damn fools wouldn't listen."

"Listen? What the hell is going on?" I asked, my hands still trembling.

Vern turned forward looking at the road ahead. "We have experienced a CME that has knocked out the entire power in the town, probably the entire country too."

"That part I get, I'm on about those freaky ass, tongue-flinging, bloodsucking—"

"Alien parasites?" Vern cut me off before casting a glance over his shoulder.

"Parasites?"

Vern took out a cigar from his top pocket and cracked a Zippo lighter open. Smoke billowed around his face and back towards us. "Well, that's our best guess right now. Until we can get our hands on one, we're kind of going off a theory."

"Which is based on?"

He sniffed. "Surveillance and research."

My brow knit together. "You want to explain that in English?"

Vern tapped thick ash on the floor. "Bryce."

Axl took a deep breath and turned. "A week ago, we had a meteor shower. I know, fairly common, however, having the CDC show up and secure the perimeter — not so common."

I thought back to the news on TV. I recalled seeing men in white hazmat suits at the impact site. The wind blew Axl's hair around and he had to speak louder in order for us to hear him. "So, we did a little digging around. By we, I mean, my father knows a few people, who know a few people that were able to confirm that the CDC was there in response to a previous meteor shower that occurred back in the '80s. Seems like a lot of people in a town in Arkansas, got real sick. A family there displayed, what might be called... unusual behavior." He stared intently at me. "Anyway, they isolated, quarantined and took the critical steps to ensure it didn't get beyond that small town. Since then, a branch of the CDC has shown up at every meteor shower."

"Because they think it's contaminated?"

"You got it."

I remembered what gramps had said was the reason behind them being there.

Axl continued. "It seems that an astrobiologist from NASA's Marshall Space Flight Center discovered what he believed was bacteria in the Arkansas meteorite. A parasite of alien origin." He sniffed hard. "If I had my computer here, I'd show you a photo of it." He shivered. "Nasty shit." He sucked air between his teeth. "Basically, under a high-powered microscope a portion of that meteor had these things which looked like tiny worms. Now I'm no scientist but think about it, we get a meteor shower a week ago. The CDC shows up. But who discovers it first?"

"Blake Davis," Anna muttered.

"And his band of merry men." He sighed. "That's right. A day later these four assholes start inviting everyone and their uncle out to these parties in the middle of nowhere. Now I've heard about folks doing a 180 and turning their life around but we are talking about four of the most narcissistic jerks to have graced the corridors of Grand County High. One moment they're keeping everyone at arm's length, the next everyone's their cheerleader? Please. Give me a break. Then we have students vanishing. No one is batting an eye in town. It doesn't take a genius to realize what's going on here."

Axl eyed his father who was watching with boyish wide eyes.

"And what is that?"

He scoffed then pretended to ring an imaginary bell near my ear. "Ding, ding, Logan Matthews. Class is in session. This is a full-on takeover. Some serious undercover shit. We are talking *Invasion of the Body Snatchers*. An infiltration of the mind, body and soul, on a level we haven't seen since Bieber mania. A parasite that doesn't just feed on us, it picks and chooses who's going to become one of them, and who's going to become a fucking human shish kabob."

We stared at him, trying to come to grips with what he was saying. In a weird way it made sense and I might have swallowed it down without hesitation, except it was coming from him.

I shook my head. "This is—"

"Crazy? Is it?" He narrowed his gaze. "Dad, you want to talk sense into this fool? Cause I've exhausted this tank."

He turned and looked at me, blowing cigarette smoke my way. "Look, kid, I know it's a lot to take in but at a bare minimum you've got to believe we are not alone in this universe, right?" He paused for effect. "Hell, it would be a waste of space if that were true. Now, I know what you're thinking cause everyone thinks the same — that if aliens existed, they would be like us, human, or green, or worse, mechanical and with death rays that shoot out of their eyes. But that's all bullshit. Get that Hollywood stuff out of your head. The fact of the matter is what we are dealing with here is a hell of a lot scarier and realistic. It's an epidemic caused by a parasite. Plain and simple. You got that?" He studied me as if waiting for a reply. "Now if you can't make sense of that, I'm not sure there is much else I can say to make it clearer. Perhaps your grandpa can."

"I'm sure he can," I replied tossing a strained expression at Anna who was sitting still, gripping my hand. The fact was it didn't take a far stretch of the imagination to accept alien parasites intruding into our world as plausible. As a species we had been fighting different forms since the beginning of time; bedbugs, scabies mites, loa loa worms, paralysis ticks, guinea worms, chigoe fleas, roundworms, Ascaris, screwworms and tapeworms. And those were just a few from our own planet that had wreaked havoc and taken lives; who knew what existed out there in space or what damage or evolutionary change they could do to the human body and mind?

* * *

When we arrived in Moab, Vern had Bones take us to his

store. All the while I kept telling them we needed to go back. In the chaos of the moment, all I could think about was escaping, getting far away from that place but now the reality was setting in. The thought Zac was still out there, scared, alone and possibly even dead sent my mind into overdrive.

"There is no going back, kid," Vern snapped. "I hate to be the one to tell you but we are in the shit storm of the century. We've got to think about survival on multiple levels. This isn't just about riding out some solar storm blackout. Those things out there will take full advantage of this event. They'll be heading for town and this time there will be a lot more of them."

The town was pitch-dark. Stores that usually were lit up even if they were closed were now shrouded by darkness. There were several residents out on the streets raising phones to the sky in some desperate attempt to get a signal. The only flicker of real light came from transformers attached to poles after they had exploded, sending smoke into the air and drenching the ground in hot orange sparks.

Multiple stalled vehicles had been abandoned in the middle of the street — doors wide open. A few drivers talked among themselves, all of them had a deer in the headlights look spread across their faces. Some pointed as the truck passed by. It must have created confusion.

Why was that truck working?

Bones gunned the motor and weaved his way around the obstacle course of stalled vehicles. Several people put up a hand trying to get us to stop but Vern told Bones to keep driving.

"How's this truck still working while others have stalled?"

"Technology, kid. The newer vehicles run on computer chips. As soon as that CME hit, it would have fried those electronics. Crazy, right? You'd think companies would think about the worst-case scenario. Nope. All they care about is advancing us into a future of dependence on the government. Now Harry, he's a smart cookie. This is a '61 International Harvester Scout. No computer chips in this baby."

The truck fishtailed around turns in the residential area until we made it onto US-191 and headed south. Planet Adventure was in Moab downtown, just south of SR-200E and across the street from Moab Diner.

It looked like it had been carved out of sandstone with sweeping curves that looked like Mexican architecture. There was a huge sign outside, and an actual inflatable boat angled down to convey a sense of adventure. Bones jerked the wheel, and the truck shot up on the sidewalk before he killed the engine.

Everyone hopped out and Vern backed up to the store with his rifle out. He raked it back and forth like he was some big-game hunter on the prowl. He tossed the keys to Axl, and he hurried over to the main doors and opened up.

"Everyone, inside," Vern bellowed. "Bryce, Bones, there is plywood out back. I want you to board up the windows."

Both of them shot off without hesitation.

Anna was now the one piping up. "Hold on a goddamn

minute. This seems a little extreme. Shouldn't we contact law enforcement? I mean the cops will—"

With his gun still trained on the road, he shot her a look. "Kid, did you not hear anything we told you? The cops aren't coming to help. They are coming to feed or turn us into one of them."

My mind was doing flips. This was too much to process. "But—"

"No buts! Blake Davis's father is Owen Davis, the chief of police. Tonight, before we saved your asses, we paid him a little visit — me, and your gramps. He's one of them, that I'm sure."

"Who, my gramps?"

"No, you idiot, Owen Davis." He thumbed over his shoulder. "Get inside."

I ran a hand around the back of my neck. "No, this is…" I staggered back feeling as if my head was about to explode. Everything seemed surreal. It was beyond strange.

"It's true, Logan," a grizzled voice came from behind. I

turned to see my grandfather heading towards us holding a flashlight.

"Gramps?"

He got this concerned look. "I know what you're going to say…"

"Do you? Cause I'm still trying to make sense of what I saw back there. You know I thought maybe, just maybe, someone had spiked my drink and this was some drug-induced hallucination — nothing but a nightmare. Because that's what it feels like."

"Harry, you want to bring the skeptic society up to speed while I get some flashlights? And make sure we have enough ammo."

Gramps saluted him. "You got it."

He put his arm around my shoulder and led me inside. His legs weren't what they used to be, so he walked with a slight limp. Out back a generator was churning away, and the room was illuminated. There was a small table off to one side, and several chairs. Gramps scooped up a bottle of beer he'd left on the table and took a hard swig of it before wiping his mouth.

"You remember when you were a little kid and used to visit with your mom and I used to tell you those stories?"

I shook my head.

"Some things are real, Logan."

"Nah, this is ludicrous. There has to be another explanation for this. Maybe it's the effect of the solar storm. Yeah, like uh, some kind of biochemical warfare that is causing mass hallucinations."

"Logan, we live on a spinning rock in space surrounded by billions of planets in one of many solar systems. There are many forms of life that exist, not all are like us. Now I don't know if these things are intelligent or what but from what we have been able to tell, they are a parasite that infiltrates the body and takes over."

I leaned back against a wall, and gramps scooped up a beer from a case on the side and handed it to me.

"Nah, I think I've had enough for one evening. I need to stay focused, clearheaded and... right now I feel far from it."

"I know it's a lot to digest, son, but you saw it with your own eyes."

I recalled it again, running through it in my mind.

"By the way, I thought you were going out for drinks tonight?"

"And we did, except it involved surveillance."

"Yeah, Vern keeps throwing that word around."

Gramps got up and walked over to a metal cabinet and rooted around until he pulled out a folder and slapped it down on the table. "Vern and I have been studying this for a long time. At first it was just research for the radio show. You know, coming up with new content and whatnot but then we saw a pattern emerge the more we looked into the activity of the CDC."

He flipped the folder open and pulled out a stack of photographs, paperwork and what looked like profiles.

"We managed to obtain from a source at the CDC these photos. Let's just say that we aren't the only ones concerned about what happened in Arkansas."

I looked down at a series of photographs and picked them

up. There were different bodies in states of decomposition. Some of them had a mark as if something sharp had pierced them. He showed me a close-up of a face where the stinger was still hanging out.

"The black eyes and the stinger are the only means of determining a human from them. And the problem is, those things don't show until they attack. So there is no real way to know who to trust and who to fear."

My brow furrowed. "Why wouldn't your source just hand these over to the media?"

"They did. The story never made the light of day. We think someone got to them before it was released."

"Who did?"

"The others. The government. Who knows?" He took another swig of his drink. "Either way, our source gave them to us hoping maybe we could get this information out to the public. But people don't believe a lot of what is heard on a radio show."

"Well that's not exactly a big surprise, now is it?" I said eyeing him. "Come on, Gramps, that is some weird shit you spout on there."

Outside the room I could hear Bones and Axl nailing in boards and Vern barking orders at them like a boot camp instructor.

"I agree, it's on the fringe and people tend to dismiss what they don't understand or can't believe without proof — and proof is scarce when you are dealing with the extraordinary. The fact is we live in a strange world, Logan. The longer I have lived the more I realize that I don't know squat about this planet, let alone what is out there in the solar system."

As I continued to thumb through photos, I came to one that showed the body of a man dressed in farming gear. His head was a short distance from his torso, and there was a stinger hanging out of his mouth.

I tapped the photo. "What is that?"

He breathed in and smacked his lips. "From what we can tell it's some form of proboscis."

"Proboscis?"

"Like the part on a mosquito that pierces the skin. It's an

extensible tubular sucking organ that's used to feed. Except in this case, we think they can also pass on parasites to duplicate themselves and slowly take over more people, no different from the way a common cold might be spread."

I stared at the photos for a few more seconds before dropping them on the table.

"Once the parasite enters, how long does it take for them to change?"

"Based on what we know from the Arkansas case, it takes twelve hours for the parasite to take control. In that time they act clumsy, confused, but are still dangerous. Within twenty-four, they become agile, able to scale walls and upside-down surfaces using some kind of stiff bristle padding like an insect."

"Is there a cure? You said they contained it in Arkansas."

"Contained, yes; cure, not that we know." His eyes dropped to the photo. "What you are seeing is how they dealt with it."

"Severing the head?"

"From what we can tell the parasite invades the brain. Sever the spinal column, then burn them alive. Anything else, gunshots or arrows, only slows them down."

I looked at him with despondent eyes. "Zac is still out there."

Gramps narrowed his eyes. "What?"

Guilt washed over me.

"I took Zac with me to the party, and uh… well… there was a lot of people there and once it went dark, I couldn't see him and… then screaming, people running and…"

The frustration was overwhelming.

Gramps got up and gripped my shoulder. "Look, we'll figure this out but first we need to get to your mother. Pick her up and…"

"No, I need to get Zac."

He grabbed a tight hold of the sides of my arms. "Snap out of it. Going back in is suicide. Our best chance of survival is to stick together. Let me go speak with Vern and we'll decide what to do next. For now just sit tight."

"What about my parents?" Anna asked.

Gramps gave a nod before he exited the room. I dropped into a seat and stared at the photos. A blackout was hard enough to deal with but this was beyond anything we could imagine. Anna paced back and forward muttering to herself. Bones came into the room along with Axl and both of them stared at us.

"You two need to gear up. This is going to be a bloodbath."

"Let's do a check," Bones said. Bones turned and attached to his back was a compound crossbow used for hunting. Tucked into a quiver at the front of it was a collection of titanium-tipped arrows. Attached to the side of Axl's leg was a sheath with a machete and on his right side was a Glock, along with multiple magazine holders attached to a duty belt. They were both kitted out in camouflage gear, the same kind they wore to school, except they were also wearing steel mesh masks that went over the lower half of their face. Once Bones was checked, he turned and checked Axl's gear.

"Okay, we are good. Ready to kill."

"Am I the only one here that is sane?" Anna said casting a glance over everyone. "I'm not killing anyone."

"Darlin', you better wake up and smell the coffee. Life as you know it has gone bye-bye. Love it or hate, this is the new reality and the sooner you man up and grow a pair, the sooner—"

Before he could finish, Anna gave him a swift kick to the nuts, and he doubled over.

"That man enough for you?"

She turned to Bones, and he tossed his hands up for a second then covered his jewels. "No beef here."

Axl groaned on the floor, muttering something about how she had ruined his chances of keeping his bloodline alive. Anna stepped over him and walked out of the room leaving us in silence. Bones tried to help Axl up, but he shoved him away and grumbled.

In the main area of the store, I could hear gramps arguing with Vern. Something about how he wouldn't let his daughter die out there. I squeezed past Bones who was going through another check of his equipment and went out to see what all the commotion was about. The main room was lit up by several wind-up lanterns positioned in different spots around the store. I was now able to get a better view of the store itself.

Everything was made from pine — the walls, the shelves and the checkout area. Beyond that were numerous racks of T-shirts and outdoor clothing. There was rafting equipment, bicycles, accessories and a complete hunting area stocked with camouflage clothing, axes, bows and rifles. In front of the main counter was a glass cabinet filled with different hunting knives, several machetes and all manner of manly gadgets. Behind the counter was a sign on the wall that read: Choose Your Adventure, and then it offered private tours, rafting, Hummer safaris, paddle boarding, climbing, hot air balloon rides, mountain biking, Colorado River jetboats, scenic flights, horseback riding, high rope courses, Jeep rentals and zip lining. It was a one-stop for everything an outdoor enthusiast could want.

"Harry, you know we can't do it."

"So you want to stay here and wait until they descend upon us?"

"No, I think we need to take stock of the situation and come up with a plan of action."

"The plan is simple. We get family and get the hell out of here, make our way to the CDC and alert them to what is going on and hope they can put an end to this nightmare before it spreads. If we are lucky, this might be contained before it gets out of control."

"It already has. Look, Harry, the CDC was at the impact site. They already know. Chances are in a matter of hours this place will be swarming with government officials. Now if you want to go out there and get yourself killed, be my guest but as a friend, I'm urging you to think this over."

"I already have." Gramps turned and motioned with his head. "Logan, grab some gear to protect yourself and let's head out. We are going to get your mother."

"And Zac?" I asked.

"First things first."

Vern gritted his teeth. "You stubborn son of a bitch." He exhaled. "Let's go then."

Gramps raised a hand. "It's better you stay here. The fewer people out there, the better."

"That wasn't a question. I'm going with you."

"Me too," Anna said. She charged over to the counter and pulled off the largest bow she could find and pulled it back like she was getting ready to perform in an archery tournament.

"Hold on a minute, Anna," Gramps said.

Right then Axl came out cupping his hands over his balls.

"You don't want to argue with her. Trust me."

Chapter 10

No one stayed behind. Convincing anyone to stay would have been a tough sell. Vern's excuse was that we needed to stock up on food and water before the stores were looted. As for Axl and Bones, well, I think they were just looking to settle a few high school vendettas.

But one thing we all agreed on. We were worried about family. There was no way to know really what was going on in the state, or how far this extended throughout the nation. The news had mentioned multiple meteor showers. Were those organisms, parasites, whatever the hell they were, only on that one meteor? Had they done this to other planets that were inhabited?

So many questions with few answers. We were all grasping at straws, going on photos from the '80s and the words of two town loons. Except now, I'd witnessed it with my own eyes.

For a few minutes, everyone argued about whether it

was wise to take the truck. With no more vehicles in operation, and the streets filled with desperate people, there was a good chance people might take things into their own hands. But jogging would have meant delays, and every second they were out there was an increase in risk. Now, I didn't expect people to go ballistic within a matter of hours of a blackout. That wasn't realistic, but with those things out there, it wouldn't take long for everyone to panic. At first they would expect the power to turn back on, minutes would turn to hours, hours into days and once they couldn't get hold of anyone, people would take to the streets, head for the police department, pharmacies, grocery stores and do whatever it took to survive. That was if anyone made it that long. With those things roaming, and zero power, there was no knowing how quickly society would collapse.

As the truck bounced along the street, heading north on Main, and then hanging a right onto east 100 I couldn't help think about the varied reactions folks would have to the blackout, never mind the horror that was about to take hold of the town.

Of course there would always be those who would believe people wouldn't take matters into their own hands, that they would work together to help each other, and perhaps they would but it would have been naïve to think everyone would take on that mindset. Frustration, stress, panic and desperation were powerful motivators in pushing people over the edge.

The hurricanes that had hit the East Coast were a prime example of that. Within a matter of twenty-four hours, store shelves were stripped of supplies, lines formed at gas stations and many even closed.

"Now listen up, we get in, we get out. The first sign of danger, and we are pulling out — with or without your mother, you understand?" Vern said while he drove like a madman. The roar of the engine piping out through a throaty muffler was loud.

Neither gramps nor myself replied to Vern.

"What about you?" Anna asked Axl. "Where's your mother?"

"She left my old man back when I was eight years of age. Took off with some biker heading for Florida. Haven't heard from her since."

"And you?" I asked Bones.

Bones's head dropped. "They were at home this evening."

"And you don't want to get back and check on them?"

"I do but we have bigger fish to fry."

Axl eyed us all and then filled in the blanks. "Bones here doesn't get along with his parents. Isn't that right?"

He didn't nod, just looked out into the darkness.

"His stepdad has a taste for whipping out his belt when he's had a few too many Jim Beams. And his mother, well, she is too damn scared to do anything about it."

Anna stared at him. "Is that why you used to disappear for several days at a time?"

"Hard to hide black eyes," Bones said. "It doesn't happen as much as it used to but every now and again he takes it out on me. Better me than my mother."

Axl leaned back eyeing us as if trying to gauge our reaction to the news.

"You never went to the police?"

"It's not as easy as that." Bones looked away as we drew near the station. I had more questions but right now my mind shifted back to the task at hand.

The Moab Police Department wasn't much to look at. A rectangular building that crouched at the edge of the road — there were no police cars outside, no doubt they were responding to situations before the power went out.

Vern eased off the gas.

A light was on in the building; backup generator, gramps said. I hopped out.

"Okay, leave the bows in the truck. Get in and out."

"Leave the bows?" I asked. "After what I saw out there, I'm not taking any chances."

"You go in there with a bow in hand, they are liable to take you down and throw you in a cell. Use common sense."

"There's no law against carrying one."

"Whatever," Vern muttered. "Don't say I didn't tell you."

Anna and I hurried towards the entrance while the others waited outside to keep watch.

"You ever fired one of these before?" Anna asked.

"Never."

"It's simple." As we jogged towards the entrance, she showed. "These have sights on them. When you draw and shoot, you center your pin and peep sight in the rear, put the pin on the target and release. Don't hold the bow like a baseball bat, otherwise the string will lay against your forearm. Have your hand turned at the eleven o'clock position. You lay your arrow on the rest, do a full draw back to your jaw, to where the peep sight lines up exactly with your eye. As we aren't using a release around the wrists, you relax your hand and the string will slip away. You got that?"

"Worse-case scenario, I can always lob the whole bow at them."

She shook her head, and we arrived at the door.

"Look, I think I should go in alone." I handed off the bow. "I don't feel comfortable heading in there looking like I'm about to go all Robin of Loxley on them."

"You heard what he said about the chief."

"Come on, do you honestly think this has made its way into the police? I'm pretty damn sure if it had we would have heard about it by now."

"From who?"

I handed off my bow. "Just hold this, if I'm not out in five, come get me."

"At least take this."

She pulled off a large hunting knife in a sheath. I took it and slipped it into the back of my jeans. It stuck into my ass as I pulled my shirt down to cover it.

"Five minutes," she said. I gave a nod and pulled open the doors and entered.

Inside there were several people sitting in chairs against the wall, a couple were at the front desk talking to a police officer and complaining about the power going out and vehicles not working.

"Ma'am, we are dealing with the problem at hand. An update will be issued once we have further details. For now I will need you to take a seat."

She slammed her hand against the counter.

"I'm not going anywhere until you tell me what is going on."

The cop turned and motioned to some other cop to give him a hand. He headed out and directed her back to her seat. I took advantage of the distraction and headed up to the front desk.

"I'm here to see my mother, she had her orientation as a dispatcher today."

"What's her name?"

"Sage."

"And yours?"

"Logan Matthews."

He eyed me with a look that put me on edge. His eyes shot over to the cop who was struggling with the woman and trying to keep her at bay.

"Okay, take a seat and I'll go see if I can find her."

He got up from the front desk and wandered off.

"Get your hands off me," the woman said. I turned and watched with curiosity as she was manhandled. A few of the others sitting there protested about the use of force. He didn't exactly have any option; she was pushing back and acting like a complete lunatic. Beyond the glass doors, I could see Anna looking in. I made a gesture to let her know I was waiting. She looked away.

Right then another officer came barreling out from the back, pulled the door wide and hurried over to assist his colleague. The door swung shut, and I heard the lock clunk. Both of them were now struggling as another member of the public got involved. While that was taking place the front desk guy returned and pressed the buzzer on the door.

"Head on in, first left at the end of the corridor, go down the stairs and take the first right."

I pushed through the door and cast a glance over my shoulder. I hurried in moving as fast as I could along the corridor and following his directions. When I entered the dispatch room, a red-haired woman was chatting to my mom. They were sitting in front of a desk with five computer monitors. The redhead noticed and gave a nod and my mother cast a glance over her shoulder.

She immediately went into mom mode, scraping her chair back. "Logan, what's going on? Everything okay?"

"There's been a blackout."

"I know. I'm running late here while the IT guys try to get things working again."

"It's not going to work again. We need to go."

I turned to head out. "Logan, where's Zac?"

And there it was, the question I didn't have any answer for, so instead I lied.

"He's at home. Not feeling well. You need to come. Fast."

She turned to the redhead. "Look, Sheila, I'm sorry but my youngest has fallen ill. I need to head out."

"Sure, no worries. I hope everything is okay."

I couldn't believe everyone in the department was taking the whole event in stride like it was just a glitch, and one that would soon be resolved. But then on the other hand it made sense. No one would have known the extent of what had occurred unless an announcement was made and I hadn't heard one that stated the CME was definite. The news was just filled with fear-based rumors — nothing more than arguments for and against. How was anyone meant to have confidence in that?

As we hurried along the corridor heading towards the stairwell, my mother kept peppering me with questions. Dropping the real bombshell on her right then would have done nothing more than thrown her into a state of panic or caused her to get angry thinking I was lying. Hell, I was still having a hard time believing any of it, and I'd witnessed things I couldn't even explain.

Suddenly, stepping out from a room off to the right, an officer bumped into us.

"I'm sorry." He glanced at my mother and then looked at me. He was dressed differently to the other cops. That's when I saw the name on the gold tag — Chief Owen Davis. "Are you leaving?"

I swallowed hard and diverted my gaze.

"I'm afraid so, chief, my son is sick, so I need to go home early."

His eyes flitted over. "So this must be…?"

My mother smiled with pride and her eyes bounced between us. "Logan, my eldest."

"Nice to meet you, Logan." He extended his hand, and I stared at it. The last thing I wanted to do was go anywhere near him. If Blake had been turned, had he done the same to his parents? According to what Vern had said, he was pretty much convinced that Owen was one of them.

"Logan, manners," my mother spat as she noticed that I wouldn't put my hand out. Slowly but surely Chief Davis retracted his hand.

"That's okay, boys will be boys."

"I'm sorry, I'm not sure what's got into him."

"Mom, we need to go," I said pulling on her wrist and edging my way around the chief.

"Nice to meet you, Logan," he said in an odd manner.

It was cold and without emotion. I was sure his lip curled up as we burst through the doors into the stairwell. By now I was practically tugging on my mother's hand to get her to speed up.

Her voice rose. "Logan, what on earth is the matter with you?"

"I can't explain but…"

Right then the knife in the back of my jeans slipped out and bounced down the steps, just as the bottom door opened and Chief Davis walked in. His chin dropped to the ground and then up to where we were. He crouched and picked up the knife, rolling it over in his hand.

"Belong to you?"

My mother's gaze darted between the knife and me. "Logan?"

The chief took a few steps forward and extended it out.

I cleared my throat before spitting out, "It belongs to a friend of mine. He gave it as a gift."

"It belongs to him or belongs to you?"

"Me."

He nodded and glanced at it again. "You like to hunt, Logan?"

Okay, his tone was freaking me out. My mouth went dry, and I felt my pulse racing. A bead of sweat formed at the small of my back.

The chief smiled. "Here, take it." He extended his hand and held it out.

I hesitated long enough that his eyes narrowed.

"You don't want it?"

Even my mom seemed surprised, and I knew she would chew my ear out on why I had it in the first place, but not collecting it? I had crossed the line between what she would let slide and what she would...

She rolled her eyes. "You can give it to me. Boys will boys," my mother said heading down the stairs.

"Mom, don't," I blurted out. The chief's gaze fixed on me as if he could read my mind. Could they read minds? If they could, could he sense fear? She ignored me and stepped forward to take it from the chief when he grabbed her by the wrist and pulled her in tight, locking his arm underneath her chin.

She let out a pitiful cry.

"Chief, what are you doing?"

He kept his eyes on me. "What are we doing? Would you like to answer that question, Logan, or should I show your mother?"

Right then I knew what was coming.

His head tipped back and mouth widened, and then like a cobra exiting a wicker basket, one of those disgusting red stingers shot out. In an instant I reacted, taking two steps and lunging feet first towards him. I collided, knocking both of them down. The knife slipped out of his grasp and rattled across the floor. I scrambled to get it and felt a meaty hand clamp down on my ankle. I stumbled and hit my knee, sending a shot of pain coursing through me. I used my other foot to kick him square in the face, once, then twice until he released my leg. But before I was within a foot of that knife, I felt my body being slammed into a wall. I landed hard and saw him rise. Using every ounce of my strength, gripping my rib, I backed away from the wall. I saw my mother had struck her head and was out cold.

"Now look what you've done, Logan."

I gritted my teeth. "What the fuck are you?"

His hand extended. "Come, I'll show you."

"Stay the hell back, man."

All the commotion had caused so much noise that a door opened on the next floor. An officer hurried down, stopping at the top of the steps to observe.

"Chief? You okay?"

Davis had his back to him. He smiled at me and retracted the fleshy needle that hung from his lips before turning to the officer.

"Actually, I'm having a little trouble with a minor here, perhaps you can give me a hand."

The officer took a few steps down.

"What happened to the woman?"

"The kid."

A smile flickered on his lips.

"Don't believe him. He's not one of us."

The chief laughed. "Oh he has serious problems."

The trusting officer bounded down to assist. Though I pleaded for him to stay back, it was too late. As he moved past the chief, his focus was fixed on me. I saw the chief's head tilt back, and I knew what came next.

The officer grabbed me hard. "Okay, kid, turn around."

"Look," I yelled. The officer turned just as the stinger pierced his throat. He let out a guttural cry. Not wasting a second, I grabbed the gun from his holster, aimed and fired a round straight into the chief's chest. He collapsed to the ground, and I ran past him and pulled my mother up.

Blood was trickling down the side of her face.

"Wake up, come on," I shouted, slapping her cheeks. My eyes darted over to the chief who wasn't moving.

As my mother came to, I slipped her arm over my shoulder and climbed the stairs. "Logan? What's..."

The crack of the gun had attracted other officers.

What occurred next happened so fast, all I could do was watch in horror.

The same two cops that had been dealing with the unruly woman burst through the door at the top of the stairs. As soon as they saw me holding my mother and the gun, they drew their firearms and yelled for me to put the gun down. I shouted back, trying to tell them what was going on, but they weren't listening.

That's when it happened.

Their eyes lifted. "What the fuck?"

They immediately began shooting. I turned my head in time to see the chief scaling the wall. No boots on, his hands and feet clinging to it like he was a fucking spider. What the hell! The attack was fast and furious. The bullets struck him but he quickly pounced on the two officers.

That momentary distraction was all I needed, I hurried past them through the doorway and dragged my mother down the corridor. The sound of feet pounding the floor behind us got louder, I turned and fired a few more rounds but he sprang from side to side, dodging the bullets. I knew in that instant we were screwed.

A few more steps forward, heading for the door.

All I could see was our escape and all I could hear was heavy breathing behind us.

In those final seconds before certain death, I squeezed my eyes closed waiting for it to be over but continuing to move forward. As I opened them, standing ahead, ten feet down the corridor was — Anna.

I heard the whizzing sound as the arrow flew past.

Then a thud from behind as his body collapsed.

I turned to see an arrow sticking out of his head, black ooze trickling down his skin.

"Holy shit." I turned back to Anna. "How did you…?"

She tapped her watch. "I didn't. Five minutes was up."

Chapter 11

As we exited the building with my mother in tow, Anna clarified further. When she saw the two officers react and hurry back into the central part of the station, she knew something was wrong. She slipped in behind them as the sound of gunshots echoed. As she explained, my mind kept rolling back to what I'd seen. The way the chief had scaled the wall like a bug. He made it look effortless but not as effortless as the way Anna fired that bow.

"That was one hell of a shot. Where did you learn to fire like that?"

She may have smiled, but I didn't catch it. The seriousness of the situation had both of our nerves on high alert. We hurried over to the idling truck, my mother pestering for answers, and answers she would get but not before we got the hell out of there.

We piled into the back and gramps hugged my mother

as Vern slammed his foot on the gas and gunned it. The headlights washed over the darkened streets, lighting up the faces of the confused, the desperate and the Vipers. That's the name we'd given them because of the way their heads flipped back before they struck with the stinger.

"You killed him?" gramps asked, his eyes widened.

"I did," Anna said. "I mean, I slowed him down."

"Girl, you have a big pair of kahonas," Axl said while keeping his distance. He knew better than to piss her off.

I leaned in through the open cab window. "Where are we heading?"

"For safety," Vern said.

Bones was experimenting with a battery-powered radio in his lap. Static hissed as he tried multiple stations, and for a while he wasn't having much luck until he finally landed on a station that was playing a message on a loop.

This is not a test. Please stand by. This is the Emergency Alert System. The following critical message is transmitted at the request of the Centers for Disease Control and the Federal Emergency Management Agency. A shelter in place warning is in effect until further notice for the states of Utah, California, Florida, New York, Kentucky and Texas. As of 9:30 p.m., there have been two hundred and forty-six known cases of an outbreak of unknown disease within the warned areas. FEMA is warning persons within the affected areas to remain where you are. Do not leave your homes. This disease is spread person to person through attacks by those infected. At this time it is expected that more attacks of this nature will occur in other states in the next few hours. The intent of attacks is unknown at this time though it is believed it is to spread the unknown disease. To protect yourselves from harm, all residents of the United States are encouraged to follow these instructions: Stay away from anyone showing signs of aggression. If you are outdoors, go indoors immediately. Let no one in that does not live with you or is visiting you. Seek shelter in a room above or below ground, preferably one that is blocked by several doors. Make sure you have taken food and water to your place of refuge. It is unknown how long this event will last but with the power grid down, the National Guard and the military are doing *everything in their power to aid those in the areas of warning. Stay calm as authorities have been dispatched to deal with those attacking. This message will be updated when the situation is under control.*

It then made a few more robotic sounds and began to repeat. Bones turned it off and looked over to Vern.

"Under control? Stay inside? Bullshit. We need to get out of this town ASAP."

"And go where? You heard it. Whatever is happening here is occurring across multiple states."

"That meteor must have only been one of several that hit," gramps mumbled.

Vern eyed him in his rearview mirror. "No shit."

"Okay, hold on here. We might be jumping the gun. You heard them. They said get inside. Help is coming," my mother said. Even I knew that would not happen with the power grid down, planes out of operation and most vehicles no longer working. It meant most of the military would be on foot unless they got their hands on some old vehicles with no computer chips in them.

Vern burst out laughing. "The government helping, now that's a novelty. Those assholes care about only one thing — themselves. Believe me, if they are coming, it's to quarantine and contain the threat by whatever means necessary."

"And we all know what that means," Bones said. "They will wipe everyone out."

My mother frowned. "What the hell are you on about?"

Bones turned in his seat as the truck rumbled along the last stretch of road towards Vern's store. "Ms. Matthews, I hate to be the bearer of bad news but the world you know has come to an end. We aren't just dealing with a blackout, but a full-scale invasion, Trojan horse style."

My mother looked at me. "The chief."

I nodded and didn't need to say any more. Just as each of us had gone through the process of trying to wrap our heads around it and letting the hard reality sink in, she too would have to ride it out.

"We will leave in the morning," gramps said.

"And Zac?" I asked forgetting that my mother still didn't know.

"What about Zac? You said he was at home ill."

"I had to get you out of there."

"Logan?" She leaned forward. "Where is Zac?"

I cast my eyes down and knew this would not end well. No matter what I said, she would explode. I brought her up to speed on what had happened and strangely enough at first, she didn't react the way I thought she might. She leaned back and stared down into her hands, rolling her wedding band around on her finger.

"Mom?"

Then, as if waiting to reach boiling point, she erupted. "How could you!"

No one on this planet could have moved fast enough to duck her swipe. The slap struck me across the back of the head and another one was right behind it, except gramps stopped her before I ended up with a mild concussion. He physically had to restrain her until she broke down in his arms bawling her eyes out.

"Holy cow, you are a feisty one," Vern said from the driver's seat. Gramps glared at him and he went back to keeping an eye on the road ahead.

"Where would we go?" Axl asked his dad.

"Anywhere but here."

"There are fallout shelters in North Dakota," I muttered. All of them looked around at me as if surprised that I would know. I assumed it was common knowledge. I'd seen a piece in one newspaper about it. It wasn't exactly a secret. The company was looking to make some serious coin by creating as many of these end-of-the-world communities as they could. Each community could hold up to 5,000 people, and each bunker was made of concrete and steel and could withstand a 500,000 pound blast, temperatures reaching 1,250 Fahrenheit, a force 10 earthquake, 500 hours submerged in water and winds up to 450 MPH, along with radiation, biological and chemical attacks. The company had established a network of these communities throughout the United States and one in Europe.

Vern shook his head. "Kid, I think we are a little late to get on the list for that."

Axl agreed. "I say we break into the gun store and stock up on as much firepower and ammunition as we can before someone else does."

"Yeah right, and the cops? They are still out there," Anna said.

Bones interjected. "They're probably Vipers by now."

"The three inside weren't. Just the chief."

Axl leaned back and pulled out a cigarette, placing it between his teeth but not lighting it. "Then it makes you wonder, doesn't it? What's the end game in all of this?" He paused and lit it.

"Well I don't think they came here on purpose."

"Arkansas a few years back, now this? Sounds like they are determined," he said.

"Who's saying they ever left?" Bones muttered.

"Still, makes you wonder, doesn't it? I mean, most parasites inhabit a host and eventually break it down. If they are using us as a source of food and yet duplicating themselves, how are they choosing who to feed on and who to turn?"

"It doesn't matter," Vern muttered as he jerked the wheel and we veered around a turn. So far the town wasn't out of control. Only those with radios, or people prepared for the worst-case scenario would have taken action, the rest would still think the power would turn back on.

"You think it's wise to leave?" Anna said. "It will not be much safer out there."

"Maybe not but at least out there we might find a town without bloodsucking freaks causing havoc. If we avoid the states mentioned in the broadcast, we stand a chance of riding this out."

"Stop the truck, stop!" Anna yelled pointing to a car surrounded by four people who were rocking it back and forth. One cracked the window with an elbow, lifted his head and a slimy stinger shot out, striking the driver.

Vern kept going as we got closer to his shop. "Sorry, kid, but…"

"I know those people," she said protesting before rolling over the lip of the vehicle while it was in full motion.

"Anna!"

There was no stopping her. I banged on the side of the truck. Vern slowed a little, and I hopped out grabbing up a machete. Anna had already hit the ground running towards the nightmare unfolding.

"Hey assholes!" she yelled.

They turned, and she fired off the first arrow and struck one in the chest sending it to the ground. As soon as that one struck she had the next one ready. The other three turned and sprinted towards us. *Oh shit!* I cringed as I brought up the machete.

They stopped running and fanned out as a few gunshots were fired overhead and one hit the ground. The other two turned and fled. *Self-preservation.* They hadn't lost it. These weren't mindless individuals taken over by a parasite with no concern for survival. It wanted to live. The two individuals that had been hit, eventually got up as if barely affected by the arrow and bullets, then scrambled away like vermin.

Within seconds it was over.

The Vipers disappeared into the darkness.

Anna hurried over to the vehicle. A woman inside was leaning over a blood drenched man in the driver's seat, holding a wad of napkins to the side of his neck.

"Please. Help," the woman cried.

"Mrs. Harris," Anna said pulling the door open.

"Anna?"

All of us assisted in getting them out of the vehicle and helping them to safety. We weren't far from Vern's store. It was a few more blocks down the road. Bones and Axl helped me hoist the guy up into the back of the truck before we peeled away.

The woman Anna referred to as Mrs. Harris was sobbing uncontrollably over her husband as he bled out in the back of the truck.

"Stephen. Oh, Stephen," Mrs. Harris said over and over again.

"Hurry, Vern," gramps said.

"I'm going as fast as I can."

The truck bounced up the curb and along the walkway before pulling around the side of the store. Frantically we dragged Mr. Harris out the back and into the store. The door was quickly locked behind us and Vern had Bones and Axl switch the generator on and get the external surveillance cameras operating to ensure those things hadn't followed us.

Mr. Harris was brought into the back room. Vern cleaned off a large oak table, and they laid him down. The bloody napkins were still clamped against the side of his neck; blood was trickling and soaking them. My mother stared on as Vern told Anna to get some warm water from the back, along with some towels.

Mr. Harris's skin had turned a pale white. Vern said it was from the loss of blood, shock, and well he didn't finish what he was saying because he was bellowing orders and cursing the Vipers.

"Stephen, can you hear me?" Vern said slapping him

on the cheek. "Stay with me."

He was making this grotesque heaving noise, his chest rose and fell fast and his eyes were closed. Anna returned and Vern pulled away the napkins against his neck, that's when we saw it. There was a small puncture wound no bigger than a quarter. It was sick. A dark mass swirled in the middle, a mixture of blood and… then it moved.

Vern stepped back.

"Oh my God. He's infected."

"What? What do you mean?" Mrs. Harris said

Right then, Mr. Harris let out a pained breath, and then his breathing became labored. His body twitched but at no point did he stop breathing.

"What is happening, Vern?" I asked.

"It's inside him. The parasite."

"Parasite? Get it out. Get it out," Mrs. Harris said.

Vern turned and walked over to a table where he'd put down his machete. He picked it up and headed back when my mother immediately got between him and Mr. Harris. "What the hell are you doing?"

"He will turn. It's just a matter of time."

"So you want to kill him?"

"When he turns, every one of us will be at risk. I can't have that."

He pushed forward but my mother shoved him back. "No. Are you out of your mind?"

Mrs. Harris flung her body over her husband and gripped him tight. "You are not touching him."

Gramps stepped forward and put his hand up to Vern. "Look, I know what needs to be done but maybe we should hold off."

"Hold off?" Vern yelled. "Now who's the one out of their mind?"

"I'm just saying we can learn from this. We don't know enough about them. Let's wait it out. See what happens. See how long it takes for them to change, see if it matches up with the info from our source."

Vern ran a hand over his head. "Oh and in the meantime give him the chance to infect us?"

"We'll tie him up."

"You won't lay a hand on him," Mrs. Harris said.

Gramps turned. "I'm sorry, Arlene, but it's for our safety."

She let out a howl, and it took three of us to tear her hands away from her husband who was still breathing heavily. After holding her back, Vern and gramps took him and placed him inside a large storeroom that was usually used for supplies. His wrists and ankles were bound, and the door was locked from the outside with a solid padlock.

Vern stepped back and looked at gramps.

"If he attacks, I'm gonna kill him."

"No need. I'll kill him myself."

Chapter 12

I don't think anyone slept that night. When the sun rose the next morning, there was a mixture of reactions from the group. It all seemed like a bad dream. Some bizarre concoction of the mind from having drunk too much, but one look at Mr. Harris and it was clear this was real. How many other towns and cities in the nation had come under attack? How many would fall? It wasn't like these things only ventured out at night, or were slow and clearly distinguishable. They were as ordinary looking as anyone else. That's what made it so terrifying. There was no way to know who to trust. Anyone could be one of them.

Bones stood at the window peering out from behind a piece of wood he'd pried back.

"How is it out there?" I asked.

"Quiet."

"You think they sleep?" Anna asked.

"If they don't, they were probably busy last night," Axl said as he walked over to a mini-fridge and pulled out a carton of milk and downed it. Everyone watched as he finished it. "Waste not, want not. I figure milk will be one of the first things to go. Come to think of it, if we are going to be heading out today, we will need to stock up on supplies, and salvage some food for the trip."

"Trip? You guys keep talking about a trip but you have no idea where we would go?"

Vern wandered out from the back room. "I told you. Anywhere but here."

"He's right," Bones interjected. "Once the military shows up here, chances are they aren't going to seal off the area, they will turn this place into a fiery furnace."

"You've watched one too many movies," Anna said crawling out of her sleeping bag. That was one upside to being in the situation we were in. The store had everything a person could want to survive in the outdoors, except food and water. Well, it had MRE's but not enough. Vern had been expecting a new shipment two days from now and with everything that had happened, that would no longer be an option. The same applied for vehicles transporting in gasoline, and food to grocery stores. The nation's system would grind to a halt and folks would have to be creative if they wanted to survive.

I bit down on a green apple and thought about the shelters in North Dakota. I remembered thinking as I read the article that it would never happen. That buying one would have been a waste of money. But at $35,000 a pop, would that have really been a waste? It was a form of insurance. God willing, no one would have had to use it but having one now would have been a lifesaver. Having some sense of security in a nation that was on the verge of collapse would have gone a long way.

"So how's our little friend doing?" Axl said getting up and heading over to the storage room. He went to open it up and his old man Vern barked at him.

"Don't open it."

"Why not? He's tied. I haven't heard a peep out of him all night. We need to see what kind of change we are dealing with in twelve hours." It had been close to that since we'd stumbled across them and witnessed the attack.

"Wait," Vern said and disappeared out into the main store. When he returned, he was holding an AR-15 and a handheld axe. He tossed it to Axl and then told him to unlock the door and pull it back. Vern stood about ten feet back from the door.

The rest of us grabbed up a weapon. I opted for a machete, Anna her bow and Bones a crowbar. I glanced towards the store area. My mother and Mrs. Harris had slept out there along with gramps while the rest of us stayed in the back room to make sure that thing didn't break through the door in the night.

Gramps climbed out of his sleeping bag and shuffled in to join us.

Vern gave a nod, and the padlock gave way before Axl yanked the door open.

A burst of adrenaline, then… nothing?

I squinted at the sight of an empty room. The binds were on the floor, and a pile of Mr. Harris's clothes, but there was no Mr. Harris. It looked as if he'd melted into the ground. Slowly, Vern stepped forward, inching his way closer to the storage room.

All of us looked on in bewilderment.

Just when he was within a few feet of the door, Vern jumped back.

"What, what?" Bones cried out.

Vern didn't reply but something had startled him. He moved in again and then cursed under his breath. "I knew it, he's escaped."

"Escaped? What? How?"

Vern grabbed a hold of Axl by the collar and pointed his rifle up to the tiled ceiling. There was a gaping hole where he had scaled up and slipped through. Vern quickly hurried towards the fire exit at the rear of the building and kicked it open. It swung wide and the bright light of the morning streamed in. He twisted around and circled around the store looking at the roof, but it was hard to see as there was a lip that curled up.

"Sonofabitch!"

He turned, charging back in.

"Okay listen up, he's gone. Now we…"

Before he could finish what he was saying, Bones was pointing into the main store. Vern edged his way around to see what he was looking at it. That's when we all saw him.

Mr. Harris was down on the ground holding his wife around the neck. My mother was unconscious a few feet away on the floor. Panic crept up in my chest. Had he killed her? Turned her? Mr. Harris was naked except for his underwear.

"Step away from her," Vern said while keeping his firearm trained on him. Mrs. Harris's tears streaked her face. She was unable to let anything out except for a groan as he had his forearm tight around her neck.

"Why fight? You can't win," Mr. Harris said in a relaxed voice. "It's only a matter of time until we spread across this planet. Just surrender and we'll make it as painless as possible."

"Why are you doing this?" I asked, curious to know

more about this parasite.

His eyes bounced. "You're a strange species. Always in need of answers. So unsure of yourselves."

"I said step away," Vern repeated himself.

Mr. Harris made a sick slithering sound with his lips, eyeing him with contempt, then as his mouth began to part he kept himself tucked behind Mrs. Harris who must have been absolutely petrified. Vern kept his rifle trained on him, his finger twitching near the trigger.

"You're too late, she's already changing."

In that instant, Mr. Harris released her, and she collapsed to the ground. With lightning reflexes his body leapt into the air, clinging to the ceiling as Vern fired off a round. He scuttled along the ceiling like a nasty bug until Vern and Anna fired at him and Mr. Harris dropped to the ground with a bone-crunching thud.

If that wasn't enough, Axl rushed in and brought the handheld axe down on his neck, once, twice and then a third time until he was decapitated. There was no hesitation.

All of us stepped back as black blood oozed out of the head, along with several dark-colored slugs.

"Bones, grab me the lighter fluid off the shelf."

He darted out of the room while Vern checked over Mrs. Harris. All the while we stared on, wide-mouthed and horrified as the pool of blood spread. I hurried over to my mother and checked her neck for anything but there was nothing. No heavy breathing. No outward sign she'd been stung.

"Mom, Mom, wake up."

She groaned and her eyelids fluttered. I was trying to get her to wake up when I heard the gunshot. Jerking my head to the side I saw Vern had shot Mrs. Harris in the skull. Bones returned and Vern took the fluid and squirted it all over their bodies, then snatched a rag from one shelf and fished into his pocket for a lighter. Once it was lit, he tossed the cloth onto the bodies and set them ablaze. The fire made a hissing sound, then quickly engulfed them both. Gramps gave me a hand helping my mother out of the room before the others backed out.

"You gonna let your store go up in flames?"

"The floor is rock, it's fine. Anyway, I'm not going back in there until those things are dead."

"Um, Dad," Axl said.

Vern was still talking with gramps.

"Dad!"

"What?"

"Looks like we got company."

He glanced at the video surveillance and outside it showed a group of six people heading in our direction.

"The guys from last night?"

"Might not be them."

"I'm not taking that risk. Grab what you can and let's get out of here."

We moved fast, grabbing up what was within reach before heading out the side exit and jumping into the truck. It roared to life, and we tore out just as the people we saw on video came around the corner blocking off our exit.

Vern stuck a handgun out the window.

"Get out of the way."

"Whoa, we aren't here to cause any problem. We're just trying to escape those things."

There was a moment of hesitation as they backed up and moved to one side. Vern slammed his foot against the accelerator and tore past them. I stared at a young girl who was with the group. Her eyes were red and swollen as if she'd been crying all night. A young woman put an arm around her and they hurried towards the back door. Vern had locked it, so unless they broke in, they weren't getting their hands on anything.

For a second Vern slowed down, his eyes darting to the mirror to see if they would try to steal his livelihood but Harry told him to keep going. It didn't matter now. None of it did. Life wasn't going back to the way it was.

As we drove through the town that morning, the reality of our predicament dawned on us. Several stores had already been looted in the night. We saw glass scattered across the sidewalk, a car driven through a window, a Jeep turned on its side and another burned to a husk. There were several bodies on the ground, or the remains. They looked as if they'd been drained of blood. The skin was thin and barely clinging to the bone.

Vern headed for City Market, a food store and pharmacy located five minutes south of his store. It was the biggest grocery store in Moab. There were three to be exact. It was a light tan store, with bright red lettering for the sign. It was pushed back from the road, located close to the City Market gas station.

The truck swerved into the lot and it was clear right from the get-go we were already too late. Shopping carts were toppled over, the windows of the front doors had been smashed and there were signs of blood streaks nearby. Had someone cut themselves breaking in? Or was it an attack by Vipers or an argument over food supplies?

"Now listen up," Vern bellowed. "Two of us will watch over the vehicle outside. That's me, and Harry. The rest of you are to head in and gather whatever you can. Remember, stick with the basics."

"That's if there's anything left," Bones muttered

hopping out the back and stretching. We weren't the only ones out on the streets that morning. The town was far from dead. Several wandered in groups, hurrying from one building to the next — a look of fear painted on their faces. A couple had rigged up a small kids' trailer to the back of a bicycle and was carting away several cases of water. The door on a cop car parked nearby was wide open as if they had left in a hurry.

"Now move it!"

One by one we geared up and headed into the darkness of the store. As the power had been off for over twelve hours, what little produce was left had begun to wilt in the summer heat. The beginnings of a rancid smell lingered in the air. It wasn't empty inside. The silhouette of others moved among the aisles grasping for whatever they could stuff into a cart, or carry with two arms.

Water?

That shelf was empty.

It was a given. People had been known to survive a month without food but water, a person was looking at three to five days depending on body temperature and sweating.

The residents we saw said nothing. Their eyes reflected the same story as ours — confusion, fear and desperation. We each took an aisle, grabbed a cart off the floor and zipped down them shoveling in what little remained: beans, ramen noodles, bouillon, hot cocoa, peanut butter, salt, crackers, rice, honey and canned goods.

None of us were preppers. Sure, gramps and Vern had taken a few steps to prepare themselves to survive outdoor living but even they weren't the typical survivalists — most ordinary people weren't.

As I piled a few cans into the cart, a nervous woman came down with a young girl. She was clutching her hand and eyeing the shelves. She saw what I had taken.

"You have anything?" I asked.

She shook her head. "We barely had enough food to make ends meet when there was food on the shelves." Their faces were dirty, and they both looked as if they had spent the night running from attackers.

No one could have told me how I would feel when faced with a situation like this.

Of course there would always be the so-called experts, the assholes who had an opinion about what was smart and what was stupidity. Hell, my gramps said if he had a dime for every one of those knuckleheads he'd encountered, he would have been rich.

I cast a gaze down at her child, nodded and then reached into the cart.

"Look, here, take this. Hold out your arms."

I gave her as much as she could carry. She thanked me and her little girl gave me a sweet smile before they hurried away. I stood there for a moment longer contemplating what we were doing. It was survival, that was for sure but how much of our own survival in the days and months ahead would depend on each other? Who would determine who should live and who would die?

These were just a few of the questions churning over in

my mind as I continued down the aisle and rejoined the others. For a minute or two I felt good about helping the woman until I heard her scream.

Chapter 13

I turned my head towards the screaming and hurried back up the aisle. As I reached the end, I spotted them. One of them was feeding on the young woman's child while the other two were toying with the woman. The cans of food I'd given were now scattered all over the floor, one rolled close to my foot.

It was too late for her daughter but her — those assholes weren't going to turn another one. I pulled out the machete from its sheath, sliced open a huge bag of flour on the shelf, then picked up the can of potatoes by my foot and lobbed it in their direction.

"Hey assholes."

Their heads jerked towards me.

"Come on!"

One of them broke away and came rushing forward. I stood there waiting, my pulse racing, my hand behind my back gripping the blade. The guy was in his mid-thirties, well dressed, in a pair of shorts and crisp shirt. He was almost on me when an arrow whizzed through the air striking the other one toying with the woman. The arrow punctured the side of his head, and he collapsed to the ground. The one heading towards me turned for a split second and I used that momentary distraction to lob the bag of flour at him. It burst from where I'd sliced it and the air was filled with white powder. I exploded forward, sliding across the heavily waxed floor on my knees and slicing the back of his legs, essentially hamstringing him. He let out a loud cry and collapsed to the floor.

Not wasting a second, I was up and drove the blade down into his back, before yanking it free and following up with several hard whacks to the back of the neck until his head was decapitated.

My hands trembled, and my eyes widened in shock.

I didn't matter that he'd been changed — I'd killed a man in the most brutal fashion possible. A thud sounded behind me and I turned to find Bones and Axl finishing the third guy with an axe and tire iron. They had literally pulverized his skull into fragments. By the time it went silent in that store, the floor was covered in black blood. It was a horrific sight.

The mother of the child rushed towards her baby but it was too late.

Anna kept her back with the help of Bones.

"It's not her anymore. She's dead."

They'd drained the child.

"No. NO!" she repeated over and over again, her cries of anguish echoing loudly. Other residents in the store looked on helplessly, some guy vomited at the sight. No one was prepared to see this kind of brutality.

Vern came rushing into the store. "What the hell?"

"Let me guess, you didn't see them slip by you?" I muttered.

"Actually, smart-ass, we have a problem of our own. We need to go. Now!"

I hurried back to the cart and raced out of the store along with the others. Anna tried to get the woman to go with them but she wouldn't listen. Instead, she clung to her child, appearing to want to die with her.

"Anna!" Bones yelled.

Our minds were so preoccupied by what had just happened that we didn't notice the large group heading towards us. When I glanced at them and did a quick headcount, at a guess there had to have been over fifteen. Now to anyone looking on, they might have just thought they were angry residents, except the lower portions of their jaws were covered in blood.

Gramps fired as they rushed forward, like a tide heading for shore.

Vern handed his AR-15 to Bones and then hopped in to start the vehicle. The engine growled to life as Bones unleashed a flurry of rounds in a wide sweeping fashion. It was enough to make them fan out. Several were struck in the chest and hit the ground, others sought cover.

The smell of burning rubber dominated as the truck tore through the crowd, knocking them down like bowling pins. A man reached out and my mother whacked him across the face with a hammer. We tore away, leaving them chasing after us until they became specks in the distance.

Upon returning to Vern's store, Planet Adventure, we knew we weren't going to be able to stay there. Smoke billowed from the rear, a swirling mass of black and gray. All the windows had been shattered, the plywood torn away and most if not all the merchandise in the store dragged out across the lot.

"You bastards," Vern said as he brought the truck up alongside the store and hopped out, leaving it to idle.

"Dad," Axl hollered but Vern wasn't listening. He raced into the store, followed by everyone except gramps and my mother. The inside had been vandalized beyond recognition. Someone had taken spray paint and plastered curse words all over the walls. The back section of the store had been set on fire.

Vern traipsed over clothing and picked some of it up, then dropped it.

"My entire livelihood."

Axl stepped forward to console him. "Dad, we can

start again."

"Start again?" he scoffed. He sneered and his gaze drifted around the room. A look of rage filled his face, and he balled a fist and plowed it into the drywall. "They will pay for this."

"Forget it," Anna said. "I need to make sure my parents are still alive."

She walked out and went back to the truck as Vern looked on with a long face. Axl placed a hand on his shoulder. "C'mon, Dad, it's okay."

I don't think it was the loss of goods that bothered him, it was the loss of identity. His entire life had been wrapped up in that store and to see it all swept away overnight must have been tough.

Back in the truck, an argument had ensued between my mother and Anna regarding priorities. My mother wanted to go home to see if Zac had returned, but Anna was telling her there was no point. The chances of him being alive were slim to none, and right now she needed to head over to the hospital and find out if she still had a mother.

"You don't know," I said interjecting. Anna whipped around. "He could still be alive."

"Come on, Logan, you saw how many of them there were out there. Where could he have run? He's gone. The sooner you realize the sooner we can deal with the situation at hand."

My mother shook her head and gramps tried to console her.

The tension was thick.

"Look, we are five minutes away from Moab Regional. I'm not saying we shouldn't go back to your place, Mrs. Matthews. I just need to know my family is safe."

I looked at her, then my mother who was weeping.

"Five minutes. That's all, and then we are out of there. For all we know that place could be crawling with Vipers," I muttered.

She nodded, not wishing to argue any further. I hopped in the back and sat across from my mom. Vern looked deflated as he slipped into the driver's side and revved the engine a few times before heading north. We drove up Main Street, turned left on 100 south, and continued north until we hung a left on Williams Way.

The hospital was a low-slung complex that looked more like a high school. Across the road from it was a residential area with uniform houses and behind it were sandstone foothills and mountains. When we pulled into the loop outside the main entrance, there were several ambulances there with doors wide open, a cop car nearby and a trail of blood leading away behind the building. It looked like someone had been attacked after they opened the doors on the ambulance.

That's when we saw them — the bodies — one after the next.

A grotesque display of the Vipers' handiwork.

Several weren't drained of blood but dead for no other reason than maybe they had tried to stop them. A police officer lay face down in a pool of sticky blood just inside the hospital entrance. His gun was gone. Not far from him were two security guards; both had been impaled into the wall with steel rods.

I kept a solid grip on the machete.

Axl had his old man's AR-15, and Anna was on the ready with the bow as we pressed in. A scream echoed, but it was hard to tell where it was coming from. The hospital was like a maze of corridors. We couldn't tell if it was someone in trouble or one of them trying to lure us in. The carnage only got worse the farther we went inside. Nurses' limbs stuck out from doorways, a doctor's head looked like it had shrunk from a loss of blood. We stayed silent and ran at a crouch from one door to the next with Anna leading the way.

Anna seemed to know where she was going. Every turn down a new corridor presented more horrors. There were hospital patients hooked up to machines in rooms off to the side that didn't stand a chance. It looked as if those things had been on a feeding frenzy throughout the night. Of course they would have come here first, to a place where people were at a disadvantage. I paused at a doorway unable to believe my eyes. Hanging out of a bed was a girl about seven years old, her frame, or what was left of it had been drained of blood to where she looked more skeleton than human.

"Dear God."

"Logan," Anna muttered standing at the corner. I hurried over to her and then saw what she was looking at. Farther down the next corridor were two Vipers feasting upon some poor soul laying on a gurney.

"Any other way around?"

She gave a nod, and we quietly backed away.

Avoidance was the best tactic we had. Fighting for the sake of it was a risk none of us wanted to take. One slip. One wrong move, and it could be over.

We moved fast, hugging the walls with our backs and being on the ready for anything. Anna led us through another series of doors until we looped around to where we would have been had we gone the other way.

She stopped outside a door and quickly opened it. It was your typical office. Nothing fancy. The only thing that distinguished it as her mom's was a photo of her family on the desk, and a gold plaque which had the words: Doctor Michelle Campbell.

She looked a lot like her mother — dark curly hair, and Pacific blue eyes — a woman that looked after her health and enjoyed life, if the smile on her face was anything to go by. Her father looked stern. He had a bald head, and small glasses and looked like your typical middle-aged father — kind, yet embarrassing.

Anna turned and headed back out the door. I grabbed a hold of her. "Anna, you know she might not be here."

"I have to find her. There's one other place I want to check."

A look of anxiety spread across her face. I gave a nod, and we continued on, going room to room, taking in the sight of the bloodshed and remains. We entered a section of the hospital normally used for emergencies. According to Anna, the hospital was divided into zones and color coded, to prioritize patients based on urgency. We now moved at a fast pace through the red area. At the heart of each zone was a circular office area for nurses and doctors to coordinate, manage and keep records.

Everywhere we turned, it was a bloodbath.

Some of the nurses were on the floor, others slumped over their computers.

The way blood had been sucked out of them, it made the deceased look older than they were. One woman's eyes had shriveled inside her skull, another, the bones in her hands were visible.

Paperwork layered the floor, gurneys had been rolled on their side and all manner of hospital equipment lay in ruins. One victim had an IV pole jammed straight through his gut.

I could see the fear in Anna's eyes as she barreled through another set of doors and into an area used for surgery. There, she stopped and looked down at a figure just out of view. The person's face wasn't visible but her blue surgical gown and lower half of her body were.

Anna lifted two hands to her face as she rounded the gurney and gazed down.

"No!" She let out a scream and dropped to the floor. It

was her mother. She moved her hand forward as if wanting to touch her face but instead laid her head on her chest and sobbed uncontrollably. There was no coming back from that; her body was drained of blood.

Bones and Axl stayed at the door keeping a nervous eye out for trouble — every few seconds they would look our way. It was clear they were in a hurry to get out. I couldn't agree more. Lingering wasn't good. Not now. Not anywhere.

"Anna," I said, placing a hand on her back. "We need to go."

"Just leave me."

"I can't do that."

"Just leave me!" She yelled hard, turning away, her face red from tears streaking down.

"Keep your voice down," Bones muttered. He tucked his tire iron into the side of his waistband and pulled off the crossbow from his back. "You want to get us killed?"

"I don't care anymore," Anna mumbled.

"Anna. Do you want your mom to have died for

nothing?" I asked.

"What?"

"You heard."

She shook her head. "No, but... you heard it yourself. Even if we get away from this town, there are more of them out there. They are duplicating faster by the day. Spreading far and wide. There is no way we can survive this. Not now."

"I never knew your mother, or what she was like but I'm damn sure your mom wouldn't have given up."

"I'm not my mother."

I was about to say something but held my tongue.

"My father is probably dead too."

"You don't know."

"Even if he's alive, it won't matter because eventually they will catch us. Maybe not today but eventually."

Axl pulled away from the door, keeping his rifle low. "Fuck me. Seriously, darling, you need to nip that pessimistic shit in the bud. People are dead, you're alive, so be grateful and get up off your ass and let's go," Axl said before looking back out through the door window.

She shook her head, unable to summon the strength to argue with him. "I don't care."

"No you care, otherwise you wouldn't be here now," I replied.

"That was before. Before they killed her."

"So, don't let them get away with it. Come on. I hate to admit it, but Axl's right. You're still alive, that counts for something."

I held out my hand, she clasped it and I helped her up. Anna brushed herself off and then grabbed a sheet that had been used on a patient and covered her mother's body. She said a quiet prayer under her breath before grabbing up her bow and turning towards the exit.

"Okay, let's go."

Bones jerked his head towards us. "Actually, guys. Let's not."

Both of them hit the floor and motioned for us to get down.

From beyond the doors, we heard several boots

pounding the waxed corridors. It was them. They were out there, probably responding to Anna's scream, and no doubt ready to kill.

Chapter 14

Sweat trickled off my brow as we hid behind the surgical table. The footsteps were getting closer. A door opened, then closed, and we waited until it was silent before stepping out.

"Bones? Axl?"

There was the sound of metal sliding and then the two of them appeared from behind equipment. Bones had a bloody hospital gown draped over him. He tossed it to one side, and we didn't waste another second getting out of there.

"I want to check on my family," Bones said. I shook my head. This was not going well. We hurried down the corridor making our way out to the truck. The sound of a nearby scream put all of us on edge.

"I thought you said five minutes?" my mother barked at me.

"We got caught up."

"So? Did you find her?" Vern asked.

Anna dropped her chin, and that answered that.

"Look, I think we should split up. Bones wants to make sure his mother is still alive and well you should probably head back to the house and see if Zac has returned."

"You don't want to come?" my mother asked.

I looked off towards the hospital, still nervous about the fact that there were Vipers inside.

"No, just drop us off at his place and head back. We'll meet you there."

I hopped in and my mother looked at me and frowned. "No, Logan. I won't lose the two of you."

"I'll be fine."

She knew I wouldn't change my mind, so she didn't bother to hassle me any further. As we drove away from the hospital, I looked at Anna staring at her bow. She was shaking her head ever so slightly. It would become the norm. We knew it. The chances of humanity turning the tide now were slim under these conditions. Maybe if the power had been up. Maybe if the military were here, but that wasn't to be.

Bones continued to mess around with the radio to see if he could pick up any new updates on what was being called an outbreak. This was no outbreak; it was a takeover, plain and simple. An alien epidemic. No one was getting up from the dead. People either died or turned, it was as straightforward as that.

Scotty Moore, aka Bones lived west of the hospital in a rough-looking neighborhood called the Portal Vista Loop. It was just off W 400 North and parallel to Riversands Drive. Along the way we saw many residents. Vipers? It was hard to know. Not all of them would have had blood dripping off their chins. The fact was we couldn't trust anyone. There was no telling if someone had been turned until they unleashed that sick-looking stinger of theirs. I called it a stinger because after seeing it penetrate those at the party that night, it looked like the kind of thing that a mosquito or a wasp used to pierce flesh, except it moved like a snake and had a flesh color to it, similar to a tongue.

As we got closer, Bones looked nervous. He was twitching in the front of the truck and dialing back and forth over the same stations.

"For God's sake, Scotty, turn that damn thing off," Vern bellowed. He switched it off and put it down between his seat as we veered into the driveway. It was big. There was a black sign out front that said RAY'S WRECKERS.

"Your stepfather uses your home as a wreckers yard?"

"Yeah, nice, right?" he said in a sarcastic manner. "This was all green until that asshat tore it up and had it paved. You know, my mother had big ideas when she bought the place. Big dreams and he crushed them all. I asked her why she stayed with him and she said that despite his taste for lashing out beatings, he was a good man underneath it all." He scoffed. "Good man. She didn't want to say she was shit scared of him or maybe she was scared of living alone."

"Some women are like that," my mother piped up. "In all the years I've worked in dispatch I've heard it all. He's never done this before, or I made him angry, or I should have known better."

"Isn't that called Stockholm syndrome?" Axl asked.

"Something like that."

Vern brought the truck to a halt and Bones hopped out along with Axl and myself.

"Look, take the others home and we'll catch up later."

"How are you going to get across town?" gramps asked. "I don't think this is a good idea, Logan. We can wait."

"No," I shook my head casting a glance at my mother. "We'll be fine. Besides, idling out here is just going to attract attention."

I slapped the side of the truck and Vern muttered something to Axl before they pulled away leaving us in a plume of dust. I saw Anna look back then the truck stopped. She hopped out, and they took off. She jogged over.

"Well come on, let's go."

She charged ahead, and we looked at each other for a

second, then followed her. Bones tried the door, but it was locked. He then dropped from the steps and dug around in the dirt until he retrieved a key.

He let himself in and called out to his mother. "Mom!"

There was silence. We went from room to room searching but there was no sign of her. Bones raced down into the basement and kept calling out to her. But she was nowhere to be found. The home inside was in a mess. I thought someone had broken in but Axl said it was always like that. They weren't exactly the family that took the time to clear up.

"Maybe she's in the garage out back," I said.

He pulled back the sliding doors and hurried out calling to her.

Outside it was quiet. Not even the sound of birds could be heard. A hard sun bore down on us making my shirt stick to my back. The backyard was filled with all manner of discarded vehicles. Some had no tires, others were up on bricks, but most were gutted.

Axl motioned with the tip of the barrel. "His old man sells off the parts to used car dealerships."

"So you've met him?"

"When he's sober or when he's drunk?" Axl asked.

"Both."

He nodded. "He's an asshole. Bones spends more nights at my place than here. He only comes back once in a while to see his mother and make sure she's okay. As soon as he turned eighteen, he moved into our basement."

"And his mother?"

Axl sniffed. "I told him, if she doesn't understand the dangers of living under that guy's roof, then she has to learn the hard way."

I shook my head. I still couldn't wrap my head around the idea that a woman would stay in an abusive relationship but apparently it was common.

"But how's he got away with it for so long?"

"It happens. People fall through the cracks in the system. Child welfare overlooks stuff. Police are too busy dealing with other issues, paperwork goes missing. Ray has his fingers in more things in this town than a wreckers yard. Believe me. He has connections. He runs a storage business just south of town. Seems he does favors for several folks in…" he made a quote gesture with two fingers, "… high places."

"But still. They wouldn't overlook abuse."

"Bones is considered the boy who cried wolf. He doesn't have exactly a clear track record. He's been known to lie. He'd run away numerous times before he turned eighteen. He's had run-ins with the law on more than one occasion for stealing. It's his word against Ray's, and the side that Ray shows to this town versus the one he shows behind closed doors is very different. And it doesn't help when his mother backs Ray up. Only on one occasion did the cops pull him in and somehow he smooth talked his way out of that with a bit of community service and some anger management classes."

My brow furrowed. "But why back him up?"

"Fear."

Bones sprinted over to a huge garage that apparently

was used for car repairs, a business that Ray had owned for many years prior to meeting Bones's mother.

There was a large red sliding door, the lock was off and it was partially open. Bones pulled it back and shouted but got no response. He came back out and shrugged.

"Maybe they left, you know, took off in his truck, I don't see it here."

Bones rushed past them without saying a word. He ducked back into the house and we followed. Inside he was rooting around in one of the bedrooms. I made it to the door and watched him feel around inside the closet.

"Bingo!"

He pulled down small a black case and tossed it on the bed before popping it open. Inside was a Glock with a laser sight. He left it there and went back into the closet and continued to fish through clothes until he found several boxes of ammo.

"Was that Ray's?" I asked.

He made a noise under his breath to acknowledge before filling a magazine with bullets and slapping it into the bottom of the handle. Next he held it at the wall and turned the laser sight on. A red dot appeared, and he closed one eye. "Perfect."

"You know how to use that?"

"Sure do, and it beats a tire iron and a bow, but I'll use both. I'll certainly feel safer with this."

When he was done filling up his pockets with the remainder of the bullets, he headed into his bedroom and took out a duffel bag and loaded it up with a few clothes. He eyed keys on a rack and grabbed a set and tossed it to Axl.

"Right, let's get the hell out of here."

He charged off towards the front door without another word.

Did he care where his mother was or was he just there for the gun? He certainly didn't look lost without her. We followed him out and were about to leave when a male voice called out. It was rough, like he had smoked one too many cigarettes.

"Where the fuck are you going?"

I turned to see a large man, he had to be at least six four. His biceps were huge, as was the rest of his body that was causing his army shirt, and jeans to bulge.

His eyes narrowed. "I said, where the fuck are you going?"

"Fuck off, Ray!" Bones said ignoring his question and heading towards a small carport where an old-style truck was. "Where's my mother?"

"She's next door. Yeah, I heard you over here and thought someone was breaking in. There's a lot of weird shit going on in this town. Your mother's worried, Bones."

He continued walking forward even as Bones produced the Glock.

"That's mine."

Bones glanced at it. "Not now."

"Come on, hand it over. You know you shouldn't play with big boy toys."

Bones sniffed and lowered the gun to his side. "Go get my mother, Ray."

Ray stopped in his tracks, a look of defiance on his face. "Did you not hear me, boy? I said hand me the gun."

"You want it?" Bones raised it up at an angle as if he was some kind of gangster. "You don't get to tell me what to do anymore. Now I won't ask you twice. Go get my mother."

"You little fuck."

That was the wrong thing to say. Bones squeezed the trigger and fired a round into Ray's thigh. He collapsed to the ground, his hands covering his leg, turning to one side and crying out in agony as Bones headed towards the next door neighbor's house.

Ray cried out, "I'm gonna kill you."

Bones ignored him and broke into a jog, pushing his way through tall reeds that divided one house from the next. We took off after him. I glanced at Ray for a second, his back was turned.

On the next plot of land, the house was similar; one story, white clapboard siding and partial brick. Bones didn't wait, he hurried inside the house and before we could make it in, two shots rang out.

"Go. Go!" Anna shouted.

We hurried in to find Bones with his arm outstretched and a woman lying nearby. A stinger protruded from her mouth. She had two holes in her body, one in the head and one in the chest.

"She was one of them," he muttered in shock.

I realized in that moment and turned to check on Ray. No sooner had I wheeled around than I was launched down the hallway with such force it knocked the wind out of me. My body slammed into the wall, and for a few seconds I was dazed by the impact. Yelling ensued. Pure chaos, then a gun went off, followed by a thud as Ray collapsed to the floor, black ooze seeping from his skull.

Bones walked over to him and fired two more rounds into his skull.

Axl came over and gave me a hand up. "Shit, Logan, you took one for the team there."

"Yeah, next time, maybe you'll take a turn being a

human rag doll."

I groaned as I held my ribs. It felt like one of them was fractured.

He grinned, before turning his attention back to his friend.

"Bones, give me the gun."

Bones's hand was trembling. Viper or not, having to kill one's own mother would screw up anyone. Axl pried it out of his hands and pulled him in for a hug as if he was his own brother.

"It's okay, man. It's okay."

As we stood there staring down at the two lifeless bodies, several bloodied mucous membranes resembling slugs slipped out of the corner of Ray's mouth. They were no bigger than two inches; they slithered across the ground, heading towards us. We all quickly backed up. Off to the left the same thing was happening with Bones's mother.

"What the hell?"

Axl raised his gun and fired twice at the thing.

"No, no!" Anna shouted. "Don't waste the bullets. We need to catch one."

We continued to back up, keeping our distance.

"Catch it? Are you out of your mind?"

"You want to find out more about these? Like how to kill them?"

"We already know."

"Then why is it still moving?"

"Fire," Axl said, reaching into a pocket and pulling out a lighter. "We've got to burn the bodies." Anna grabbed his arm.

"Wait." She hurried into the kitchen and returned with a plastic Tupperware container.

"Are you kidding me?"

"Anna," I said trying to get her attention, but she was too focused. She got closer, and as she did, small tentacles came out of the side of the slug. She backed up a bit and with the lid in one hand and the container in the other, she scooped one up in one smooth motion and slammed the lid on. Meanwhile Axl had returned from the kitchen with some WD-40. He held it out in front of him and used the lighter to create bursts of fire before setting the slugs ablaze. Then he used it on the curtains. Flames instantly climbed up and set the ceiling afire as we ducked out of the house.

We didn't linger. I was certain the noise of the gun going off would attract others. We made our way back to Bones's home and over to the carport. There was a large army-style CUCV truck.

"Where the hell did you get this from?"

"These wreckers yards see a lot of old crap. Ray restored it."

We hopped in. Axl turned over the engine. It spluttered a few times but wouldn't start. He hopped out and Bones popped the hood.

"Hurry it up," Anna said.

"Unless you know anything about engines, put a sock in it."

She hit the horn and startled him, causing him to bang his head on the hood.

"Would you please..."

"Okay, give it another go."

Bones scooted into the driver's side and turned over the ignition.

It spluttered again, and he told him to hold on while he made another adjustment.

A few more seconds then he yelled, "All right."

The engine caught and roared to life. Axl hopped down from the bumper and got back in the driver's side. "That's how it's done."

"Yeah, yeah, whatever," Anna muttered. He backed out and cast a glance at Bones who was staring into space before we pulled out. Loss affected everyone differently.

Chapter 15

"Toss that thing out the window!" Axl shouted motioning to the Tupperware container resting on the floor of the truck. "We already know how to kill them and I have no interest in keeping one as a pet."

"Yeah, we know how to kill them but not without taking human life."

"Collateral damage. Nothing we can do about it."

"You're such an asshole, Axl," she spat.

"I aim to please."

"She has a point. If we knew how to fight them without slicing off heads, or setting them on fire, maybe we could have prevented Bones losing his mother. Maybe, there could be…"

"Hope for your kid brother? Was that what you were going to say, Matthews?" Axl turned his head towards me. "Cause the way I see it…"

"STOP!" I yelled.

Axl turned and hit the brakes as he jerked the wheel. The truck skidded and bounced up the curb before hitting a wall. I opened the door of the truck and stumbled out, looking back down the road to where we'd come off. In the middle of the road was a cop, his legs were injured, and he had his hand up.

"Help," he muttered. I went to rush towards him when Anna caught my arm.

"Hold on. It could be a trap."

I froze and looked back at the officer. He had a nasty gash and was holding a Glock in his hand and looking petrified.

"And if it's not? We can't leave him out here."

"Sure we can," Axl said. "Let me just back this puppy up and we'll be on our way."

"Asshole," Anna muttered again. I could see those two would get on well.

"Axl, hand me the gun," I gestured with two fingers while keeping my eyes on him.

"No, this is mine."

"Just give it."

"Take mine," Bones said handing it off.

"Really? Now you are making me look bad," Axl muttered.

Bones shrugged. I took the Glock and told Anna to keep an eye out for Vipers. Slowly I made my way over, my eyes scanning the sides of the road. Smoke rose in the distance, just beyond two homes. The sound of someone's scream filled the air.

"Please. Please."

I got within ten feet from him and kept my gun trained on him.

"What happened?"

"Help me up. I'll explain."

I shook my head. "No can do. What happened?"

He grimaced. "My partner and I were attacked by a group. We got trapped inside a building six blocks from here." He jerked his head in the direction. "I crawled out of a window but my partner hurt his leg in the fall." He squeezed his eyes shut. "I couldn't stay there. They were coming. I…"

I could see the look of guilt on his face.

"And your leg?"

"Sliced it on the window as I climbed out."

I cast a glance over my shoulder back to Anna. This was exactly what Anna was on about. There was no way of telling if he was one of them, or if this was all just some game he was playing to get me near so he could infect me with one of those disgusting slugs, or feed on my blood.

"Toss your gun over here."

"No, I need it."

"I'm not asking," I said switching the laser on and focusing the red dot on his forehead. "Do it."

He was breathing hard. "Fuck!" he said before tossing it near my feet.

I reached down and picked it up. "Can you get up?"

"If I could, would I be asking for help?"

I swallowed hard. "How do I know you're not one of them?"

"Listen, you don't but look around you, kid. Do you

think I would sit in the middle of the road all by myself waiting for a victim when there are tons of others out there that could help me take you down?"

I approached him in fear and trepidation.

"Don't do it, Logan," Axl called out. "Just shoot him."

The cop put his hands up.

"What's your name?"

"Trent Grimme."

It wasn't like I could ask him a bunch of questions and determine if it was him or the alien parasite inside him. For all we knew, if they controlled their minds, they had access to memories. Maybe they were telepathic? If so, then he knew exactly what I was about to do.

"If he tries anything, shoot him," I yelled to the others.

I moved closer and reached out a hand and he clamped hold of it. Not even once did his eyes shift. Once I had him up on his feet, he put his arm around me and we shuffled back to the truck. "Bones, give me a hand getting him in the back." The CUCV had enough room up front for three passengers if they squeezed in tight, and there was plenty of room in the back of the truck bed. Bones brought the tailgate down and we heaved him up.

"Thanks, kid."

I nodded and got back inside the truck.

"That was a dumb thing to do," was the first thing Axl said. "You could have got yourself killed and us too."

"The more people we have, the better we can defend ourselves. He's a cop. I've got to believe we can discern those who are human from those who are—"

"Not? Look how that worked for Bones."

Bones hopped in catching the tail end of what he said.

"You talking about me?" Bones asked slamming the door shut.

"Let's go."

The truck reversed out, and we took off with Axl grumbling under his breath. I took a risk but the way I saw it if I was out there laying on the ground I would have wanted someone to stop for me. Life, death, we were all clinging to a strand of hope that the country wasn't already being taken over by those parasites. Besides, I should have been dead already, back at the party.

As we were driving, Trent scooted up to the window that divided the front of the cab from the back of the truck.

"You don't want to go east on 400. It's a mess that way. We lost six of our guys within a matter of twenty minutes. Turn down 500 south."

"Are you driving?" Axl asked. "No, so keep your mouth shut and sit back and enjoy the ride."

"Axl," Anna frowned at him.

"Well I'm not going to pretend that I like picking up a stranger, especially a cop. We have enough shit to deal with without having Hopalong Cassidy with us. He will slow us down."

Anna looked back over her shoulder. "You must excuse our friend, he's a little high-strung."

"High-strung? You are carrying one of those things in that Tupperware. The town has lost power. Those bloodsucking freaks are out there. I have a right to be high-strung."

We rode the rest of the journey back to the house in silence. When the truck pulled into the driveway, outside gramps's house, the other vehicle was gone. Axl let the truck idle while we scanned the area for threats.

"You think they made it back?" Bones asked.

I pushed out of the vehicle holding the Glock out and getting ready for any sudden surprises. Axl stayed with Trent while we headed inside. As soon as I opened the door and called out to my mom, she appeared at the end of the hall.

"Mom? Where's the truck?"

"Vern took it. Said he had a few things to do in town."

There was something very off about the way she was looking at me. Anna went to walk in but I put my hand back and waved her off.

"And gramps?" I asked.

"I'm here, son," a voice came from the kitchen. I peered around and that's when I saw him — Zac.

"Zac!"

In that instant two things dawned on me; one, they

were all acting a little strange, and two, if Zac had returned that would have been the first thing that came out of her mouth. But there was no excitement, no relief.

"Come on in, don't leave the door open," she said. "I was about to put dinner on."

I frowned and my eyes darted between them.

"How did you escape?" I asked Zac.

Zac got up from the table and took a few steps towards me. "I wasn't there, Logan." He paused. "I mean, Elijah invited me and a few girls out to see some of the guys on dirt bikes a few miles from the party."

My eyes flitted between them.

"Elijah Davis?"

He nodded. I took a few steps back towards the door and with my hand I gestured for Anna and Bones to head out.

"Logan? Please. Come in. We've been waiting for you," my mother said, her head tilted to the side and I shook mine.

"No. There is no way you got out of there alive. No

way."

"Logan!" My mother was shouting now. "I won't ask you again. Close the door."

I twisted and pushed the others out, slamming the door behind me. I heard the sound of them hurrying after us. I felt the handle jiggle as I held it tight.

"Get in the truck," I yelled over my shoulder.

"Logan, it doesn't hurt. You will still be you. It's better. So much better," my brother said. Axl hadn't turned the truck off. I held on to the handle as long as I could before releasing it and sprinting. I vaulted into the back as Axl tore out, leaving gramps, Zac and my mother in a cloud of dust.

"What the hell happened?" Axl yelled from inside the cab.

"It wasn't them."

"You sure?"

I kept looking at them as we drove away. "I know my family."

I couldn't believe the Vipers had got to them. I tried to

picture in my mind what had happened. I figured Zac returned and my mother accepted him with open arms without even giving a thought to the fact he might have been infected. It would have been an afterthought. Who knows? All I knew was we needed to get as far away from there as possible.

"Where the hell do we go now?"

"Better question, where is my father?" Axl asked swerving onto the main road and heading south with no particular destination in mind.

"My mother said he'd gone into town to get something."

"Bullshit, more like he clued in and got out of there before they could go *Invasion of the Body Snatchers* on his ass."

"Where would he have gone?" Anna asked while I chewed over what I had seen. Over the past twenty-four hours we had witnessed a lot of shocking things but nothing came close to the realization that my only family had been reached.

"I say we get the hell out of here before we join them," Bones said before taking back his gun and slipping it into his waistband.

"I'm not leaving here without my father."

"For all we know, he's probably dead."

"Listen, we can go to my house," Anna said. "I need to make sure my father is still alive and it will give us a chance to think about what to do."

"Screw that, I'm heading to my house. That's where my father would have gone. He would have wanted to arm up. He has a firearms rack in the house."

"Who's saying he hasn't gone out looking for you? Who's to say he isn't already one of them?"

"I reject that. No. My father wouldn't be stupid enough to let that happen."

"Oh and my family would? Is that what you're saying?" I asked defensively.

It went silent in the truck, not even the cop in the back was saying anything. Everyone was at a loss for what to say or do. The fact was we were being pulled in multiple directions. Each of them wanted to make sure their family was safe, and yet until we found out how to kill these things without harming anyone else, no one was safe.

Axl wouldn't listen to anyone and because he was driving, he drove to his home, which wasn't that far from Anna's home on the north side of town, an area that Trent had warned us about. The streets we traveled down seemed deserted as if everyone had given up and abandoned their homes but that couldn't have been the case.

That's when we noticed residents had boarded up the windows.

"They're probably following the warning that was on the radio."

"What warning?" Trent asked.

"You didn't hear it?"

"When could I? Between dealing with the loss of power, and those bloodsucking freaks, I've barely had time to even eat. Which reminds me, I'm starving."

Axl reached into his pocket and tossed a granola bar over his shoulder.

"Here. Don't choke on it."

Chapter 16

Axl went ballistic after arriving home. Vern was nowhere to be found. He tore apart the house, kicking over furniture and plowing a baseball bat into the wall. No one said anything or tried to stop him. Loss was a hard thing to deal with but not knowing what happened to family was far worse. In some ways I kind of think after someone dies or goes missing everyone blames themselves for not saying enough, doing enough or... well... fill in the blanks, but no amount of regrets changed anything.

Whatever the hell these things were, they were taking full advantage of the town's unfortunate predicament. I even thought if America survived this and crawled back to some form of existence, I could envision talk shows discussing whether or not the CME had been caused by this alien species. Some would say it had all been part of their plan to take over the world. My thoughts? I don't think so. In my mind it was just an unfortunate set of circumstances. Who really knew except them? If they had visited our planet before and failed, maybe they couldn't deal with it and gave it another shot? Maybe they never left? They were a parasite after all. In medicine, doctors dealt with parasites in various ways, some being antibiotics. The problem is antibiotics aren't always effective. An overuse could lead to antibiotic resistance in bacteria. Essentially, the parasite would adapt to the environment, become wise to the way things work and figure out new ways to survive. *Were they learning to survive?*

"Look, I'm going to head over to my house," Anna said.

"You're not taking the truck," Axl bellowed.

"I wasn't planning on it. It's only a few blocks from here."

"I'm coming with you," I said heading out the door and leaving the rest of them behind.

"Hey, take a two-way radio," Bones yelled, jogging over and handing me one.

"Look, shouldn't we stick together?" Trent asked. We ignored him and headed off. No one would change her mind. She needed to know about her father and I wanted to be there for her in the event things didn't work out.

We hurried along the street, staying low and keeping our eyes peeled for anyone.

"It would really help if these assholes only came out at night, or looked disfigured. At least that way we could tell who was one of them and who wasn't."

"Real life is never that easy," Anna said leading the way. She had her bow and arrow on the ready. I held a machete and was fully expecting to use it.

"Why do you think they waited?"

"What do you mean?" she asked, not even looking at me.

"I mean if they arrived a week ago attached to some meteor, why has it taken them this long to attack?"

"You heard what your gramps said about Arkansas and how long it took for them to fully take over a human's body. As much as I like to think we are weak as humans, our bodies resist bacteria. Not that we win all the time but perhaps the human body puts up one hell of a fight. Maybe in those first few days it has some other agenda; to understand the host. Who the hell knows? I'm no alien scientist," she muttered. I could tell she was distracted and concerned for her father. We headed south on McCormick Boulevard, then crossed through a residential area towards her home on Sunshine Circle.

As we hauled ass, three people came into view. One of them was holding a gun, the others baseball bats. The second they saw us, the rifle went up.

"Whoa! Don't shoot," I yelled.

"You one of them?"

"If we were, do you think we would be carrying a machete and a bow?" I replied.

"How should we know? There's a lot of crazy shit going on around here."

His eyes drifted from side to side before locking on me again.

The area we were standing in was like a baseball

diamond. It looked as if it was used as a small park for the residents who lived between Hobbs, McCormick and Sunshine Circle.

"Most of the cops are dead," I replied.

"Yeah, we figured that."

"Power is out too."

"Kid, tell me something I don't already know."

The guy holding the assault rifle looked as if he was military. He was wearing camouflage pants and army boots, and even though he was talking to us he kept scanning the area. Everything about him gave me a sense that this wasn't the first time he'd been in harm's way.

Though we kept our distance he continued to pepper us with questions.

"Where you two heading?"

"Home," Anna replied, pointing towards a cluster of homes.

One of the other guys squinted and raised a hand to his eyes to block the glare of the sun. "Anna? Anna Campbell?"

"That's me."

"Hey, it's Josh Rigby."

He took off the baseball cap and pulled down the skeleton scarf mask he was wearing.

"Josh?"

She immediately lowered her bow and went to head over to them. I grabbed her by the arm. "You sure?"

"I know him from school. He's... Olivia's ex-boyfriend."

"But can we trust them?"

"Look at them, Logan. Do they look like they aren't scared? Now I trusted you with Trent. Trust me."

She walked over and for a few seconds it seemed as if the world wasn't going mad. He gave her a hug and the other guy unmasked. Slowly their faces became familiar. Josh had been in the group of jocks whereas the other guy had been part of the metalheads.

Josh motioned to his friend. "Anna, this is Richie..."

Before he could spit it out, from off to our left, three teens appeared, then from behind Josh came another two.

I twisted around and three more came into view. Wry smiles danced on their lips.

The guy holding the assault rifle immediately reacted by raising it and firing off two rounds. Josh and Richie who were both holding handguns unleashed round after round. In an instant they rushed forward, and we knew straightaway we were fucked. Their mouths opened and stingers appeared. The attack was fast and though we had the help of the three, there were too many. I sliced a stinger off and figured that if I was going to die out here, I wasn't going down without a fight. A surge of rage fueled my body into motion. Fear wouldn't paralyze me. All of us put our backs to each other as we fought them off one at a time. However, they were like rats, adults and teens appeared replacing those we took down. The look in their eyes as they lunged at us was empty. Just void of emotion.

"Go, get out of here, I'll hold them off," the military guy said firing off round after round.

"You won't survive. There's too many."

"Shit, I'm out of ammo," Josh bellowed. Richie tossed him a magazine, and he slammed it in and continued to fire as they kept coming at us. The chances of escaping were slim to none. It was only a matter of time before they ran out of ammo and even if we could hold them back with baseball bats, and a machete, it wouldn't be long before they took us down.

"We need to go." I grabbed a hold of Anna and tugged at her.

"I'm out of arrows."

"Here, use this," Josh said tossing his baseball bat to her.

The thought that I would die not because of starvation, but at the hands of some parasite pissed me off.

"Come on, you motherfuckers!"

I ran forward kicking one in the chest and slicing another across the face. Anna sprinted behind me and as I hacked into a head, she launched off my back and brought the baseball bat down on a Viper who was closing in on me. Blood gushed, and it felt like we were hacking our way through a cornfield. I stopped counting how many there were and just kept my eyes fixed on those coming at me.

Slowly but surely we carved our way through a wave of them and make our way into an alley that went down to Sunshine Circle.

"Josh," Anna cried out as two adults dived on him, their stingers striking the side of his throat. Richie shot one of them in the head but in that moment of distraction, a woman came up behind him and pounced on his back like a monkey. He swung around trying to get her off but it was useless. Once that stinger went in, it was all over. The only one still keeping them back was the military guy, and that was only because he'd pressed his back against a wall and was unloading bullets in a sweeping fashion.

Another one came at me and I jammed the machete blade straight into his mouth just as his head tilted to unleash that vile stinger.

Anna grabbed my wrist, and we bolted. Behind us we heard the cries of the jarhead as he ran out of ammo. "Come on, you bastards. You want some of this?"

I didn't turn back to see his fate, I already knew.

We hurried down the alley, the sound of boots pounding the pavement behind us, the fear of death breathing down our necks as we rounded a corner and scrambled over two stalled vehicles that were blocking the way. I felt my foot slip, and for a second my legs nearly buckled. I could feel my heart pounding in my chest, my blood rushing and ringing in my ears like a long-distance runner. We burst past a cluster of trees and were about to head down another alley when a hand came out and grabbed Anna, pulling her into an opening in a wooden fence. I ducked in after her and was about to attack when a guy put a hand to his lips, then closed the panels of wood behind us.

We heard the footsteps of our pursuers rush by. My pulse raced.

No words were exchanged; the man just motioned me

towards the back door of a home. His hand was still clamped over Anna's mouth as he practically dragged her there. As I followed him, I cast a glance back towards the fence, convinced those fuckers would find us.

But no one entered.

After stepping inside the home, we found six more people huddled together. There was a young mother and two small children, a boy and girl; an older lady in her late seventies by the looks of it; and two men in their thirties or forties. All the men were armed with knives. The door was closed behind us and blinds pulled down.

"Who the hell are you?" I asked. Though I didn't know who to trust anymore, I figured that anyone that had risked their life to save us had to have been okay.

"No one special. Just residents, like you, trying to survive."

"Mr. Bolmer?" Anna said.

"Call me Karl." He smiled and nodded as she looked around and greeted a few others.

"You know them?"

"They're our neighbors." I breathed a sigh of relief. Both of us were covered in black blood. Our clothes were a mess. Blood trickled off the end of my machete creating a small pool on the floor.

"We heard the commotion out there, and saw what was happening from the upstairs window," Karl said. "I'm sorry about your friends."

"Karl, have you seen my father?"

He gave a nod.

"Where is he?"

He cast a glance at the others and then looked back at her. He didn't need to say any more, it was obvious. Her eyes welled up and a few tears rolled down her cheeks. She'd lost everyone in a matter of less than forty-eight hours.

"How long have you been in here?" I asked.

"Since yesterday. Those things have been prowling the neighborhood attacking anyone they see. I went to help Mrs. Parsons over here whose grandson was being attacked. I've seen nothing like this. I thought the person

was sick and having problems until I saw that thing —
that…"

"Stinger," I added.

"Yeah, do you know what is going on? Is this some
kind of plague? Cause this is madness."

"Well…" I mumbled before taking a seat at the table
and laying the bloody machete at my side. "From what
we have been able to gather," I sniffed, "it's…" It was
hard to even say it as it sounded ridiculous. "Remember
this is just an assumption right now, but it seems this is a
parasite that may have made its way here on the meteors
that arrived a week ago."

"Parasite?"

"Alien."

Karl let out a gentle laugh and then his features turned
hard. "Are you screwing with me? Like *Invasion of the
Body Snatchers?*"

"Something like that," Anna said.

He let out a laugh. "So where's the pods?"

"There aren't any, at least that we can tell. It's a

parasite."

"And does this parasite have a mothership?" He chuckled.

"Listen, I know it sounds crazy but hear me out. Way back, I'm talking about thirty years ago in Arkansas, there was a similar situation to this. The CDC and FEMA were called in to contain the threat. Now from what we know, only a few people were affected before they could bring an end to it."

"The CDC? But they're responsible for..."

"Outbreaks. Yeah."

He took a few steps back and braced himself against the kitchen counter. "But, I don't recall ever hearing about that?"

"Of course you didn't. It occurred back in the '80s. There wasn't any internet or camera phones to capture images. It was easier for them to contain something like that. And besides, there was no blackout caused by a CME."

"That's what caused the power to go out?"

I nodded. I knew this must have sounded insane but what else could I have told him?

"I don't know about any alien invasion. That just sounds—"

"Crazy," I added.

"But you're saying the CDC will handle this, right?"

I chuckled. "Yes. No. Who the hell knows? From what we have been able to determine from a radio broadcast is they have done the bare minimum and alerted residents who live in six states. They told everyone to stay inside and to not let anyone in."

"Well that's convenient. We are in the middle of a blackout. We need to get supplies. We have no other choice but to go out."

"And they know that," Anna said.

"They? You mean those things?"

All six of the people inside looked disturbed, scared and perhaps even dumbfounded by what we had just unloaded on them. It was a lot to swallow in one go.

"So how do we stop them?" Karl asked.

"The humans or the aliens?"

"Both."

I stared down at the blood on my hands, could the blood change me into one of those?

"Kid."

I shook my head and tried to answer. "Bullets don't seem to stop them. They only slow them down. You have to sever the head. But that alone only stops the body. The entity or the parasite isn't dead. That you can kill using fire but unless you torch every single one that is infected, I'm not sure there is any other way."

"That's why we need to study them," Anna piped up. "I collected a sample, I'm going to head over to the school lab and see what I could figure out."

"Oh you were, were you? You barely managed to go a few blocks without losing your lives, and now you think you can get over to the school?"

"We have a truck. It works," I said.

"How? All the vehicles out there are stalled."

"It doesn't rely on a computer chip."

"So we can get out of here?" Mrs. Parsons asked. They all were waiting for an answer. I nodded.

"And where is this truck?" Karl asked.

Anna shifted her weight from one foot to the other. "About six blocks from here."

"Of course it is." He shook his head and went over to the window and peered out. "Okay, look, I'm not buying the whole invasion thing but I know for sure that some weird shit is going on, so... we can help you get to your truck but first, let's get you two cleaned up. There's no telling what that blood can do."

Chapter 17 - AXL

Trent rooted through the cupboards searching for food to eat. Mostly it was empty except for a few jars of jam, peanut butter, soup, a box of crackers and some Wheaties. I'd been racking my brain for the past forty minutes on where my father could have gone. There was only one other place he might be, and that was the store but with the fire, I couldn't see him staying there.

"What the hell did you guys live on?" Trent asked, tossing a few items on the counter.

"Shopping day was Sunday. This shit storm delayed things," I said in a sarcastic tone.

Bones looked out the window, his head shifting from side to side.

"Are they here yet, Bones?" I asked.

He looked at me and shook his head.

"Probably got themselves killed. Stupid idiots. I told them, but oh no they wouldn't listen."

"Well, maybe if you had let them use the truck."

I frowned. "First, they wanted my gun, then the truck. Do you want me to just lube up and let them shaft me too?"

Bones chuckled and went back to staring out the window. He was paranoid that more Vipers would show up and burst through the door. He'd already positioned the furniture behind the doors just in case. Trent looked like he didn't have a care in the world. He was busy making himself a peanut butter and jelly sandwich.

"Go easy on that, we might have to ration it out."

I got up and rooted around in the cupboard for some lighter fluid.

"Here." I tossed a can to Bones, along with an extra lighter. "Keep this on you. Who knows how many of those things we will have to light up."

Trent dabbed the bread with jam and cast a glance over. "I've just figured out where I know you from," Trent said to Bones. "You broke into that factory over on the west side last summer."

"Allegedly," Bones replied.

"No. I remember clearly Officer Tom Douglas bringing you into the station."

"My buddy broke the window, I just happened to be the one that got caught."

"Your buddy?" He turned and motioned with a butter knife towards me.

I frowned and put a hand up. "No. I wasn't there."

He smiled turning back to Bones. "Anyway, why did you do it? Seems there wasn't much in there to steal except a few office supplies."

"He wanted one of the computers. He believed there was a stack of new Mac notebooks inside."

"So you were inside?"

Bones stopped looking out. "Why are you busting my chops about it? I did the damn community service. Get off my case."

"Just curious, making conversation. It also seems ironic that you two knuckleheads have survived while others... who are smarter have fallen prey to whatever the hell is out there."

I leaned forward in the chair. "That's because, contrary to public opinion, we aren't idiots. Oh I know people like you think we are, just because we don't fit in with the crowd but we saw this coming long before it happened."

He nodded smiling. "Oh, you did, did you? Then why the hell are you still in this town and not fifty miles from here?"

"I could ask you the same thing."

"I'm here because it's my job, numbnuts."

"Careful, asshole," I said. "That's my food you're eating. Show respect."

"Respect?" He scoffed. "And what about you?"

"Me?" I asked.

"Yeah, you don't exactly have a clean record. Then again, the apple doesn't fall far from the tree now does it?"

"What's that supposed to mean?"

"Your father Vern. Now if there was ever a nutjob in this town, he fits the profile."

I got up and narrowed my eyes. "You want to be careful with your next words."

Trent swallowed a mouthful of food and smiled. "Um, that sounds like a threat."

"And what if it is?" I eyed him carefully, studying his expression. "Not a lot you can do about it now, is there?"

There was silence for a minute or two.

"You know, Bones, makes you wonder, doesn't it? If these things out there can blend in, who's saying that this freak here isn't one of them?"

"Sure does," Bones replied eyeing Trent.

"You two are too much. I mean why the hell did we come here?"

"To find my father."

"You honestly think your dad survived?"

I took a moment to reply.

"If anyone can survive this, it's him."

"What, because he runs an adventure shop in the day and moonlights as a paranormal investigator?" He chuckled pressing together two pieces of bread and then taking a big bite.

I got up and fished out a pack of smokes. "You think you're so damn smart, don't you? Just because you wear that uniform and have a badge, you think you're above us."

"I didn't say that."

"But you imply it with that attitude. Just remember we're the ones that saved your ass."

He laughed again. "You two guys need to ease up. Go find me some bandages so I can wrap my leg."

"Find them your damn self!" I replied jabbing the air with my finger. "You're lucky to even be alive. If it wasn't for Logan, I would have left your ass out there on that road."

"I second that," Bones said before high-fiving me.

I sniffed hard. "In fact I have a good mind to leave you here."

"That's fine by me. I mean, with such tasty cuisine available why would I want to go anywhere else?" He dripped sarcasm.

"Or better still, maybe we should tie you to a tree outside," I said eyeing Bones.

I moved towards Trent and he pulled his firearm and took a bite of his sandwich.

"Careful. This town might have gone to shits, but that doesn't mean I will let you disrespect this badge."

I scoffed. "That badge. That piece of metal don't mean shit now."

I pointed my finger at him and was about to say something when the two-way radio crackled. "Come in, Axl. This is Logan."

I pressed the button while eyeing Trent. "Where the hell have you been? I've been trying to get hold of you since — "

"Sorry, we dropped the radio."

"That's not the only thing you dropped. This fucking cop is a loon," I said before looking back at him.

"Look, we came under attack. We need you to swing the truck around. There are others here with us."

"Others?"

"Neighbors."

"Okay, stop right there. We are not picking up any more travelers. Hell, I'm thinking of dropping off the last hitchhiker and putting a bullet in his head."

Trent gave a thin smile.

"They need our help," Logan said.

"And I need beer, sex and a quarter pounder but it's not happening."

That's when her voice came over the speaker.

"Now listen up, you pinhead. Get your ass in that truck and over to Sunshine Circle ASAP. You hear me?"

"Oh, she's alive! What's it worth, princess?"

"It's worth me not blacking out both of your eyes."

"Ooohh, so cold. You know, you and I could be so much more if you just stopped trying to resist the magnetism between us. And don't you tell me you don't feel it. I've seen those fuck-me eyes."

"Eat me," Anna spat back.

"Gladly. When?"

Logan got back on the line. "Axl, just get over here

now."

The line went dead even though I cursed a few times and told them I was no one's bitch.

"Sounds like they've got you wrapped around their finger," Trent said, finishing his sandwich and giving me a smug look. I narrowed my eyes and wagged my finger in his direction.

"You're staying here."

Trent shook his head. "Come on, guys. I've got a gun."

"So have we."

"I can help."

"What, by slowing us down?"

"Think. If you're driving, Axl, you only have Scotty boy here to help you. If you come under attack, I can watch your six."

"Watch my back? Oh, that's fresh."

Bones made his way over and leaned into me to whisper. "We could use him. If we get stuck in a tough spot, we could toss him out. Slow them down."

The corner of my mouth curled. "Bones, I like your style. Let's do it."

"Do what?"

"You're coming with us."

"Really, just like that?"

"Just like that." I sniffed. "But if you slow us down, or try anything, I will put a bullet in you long before those bloodsucking freaks get their hands on you."

He smiled. "Pleasant. Remind me after this to arrest both of you."

"There is no after this," I said heading towards the door and asking Bones to check the windows to make sure there was no one coming. Once we were sure the coast was clear, we shifted out the furniture and I pulled open the door. Trent hopped over to the door, and we ducked out. We moved fast to the truck.

As we were getting in, we heard another truck coming down the road.

"Get down," I said making everyone go low. The rumble of the truck got closer and then the engine died.

While we were still low in the vehicle, there was a knock at the window. I glanced up and standing there was my father.

"Dad?"

I went to open the door and Bones grabbed me. "Hold on. Can we be sure that's…"

I looked back at my father.

"Open up," he said.

My brow furrowed. "Where did you go, Dad?"

"We got cornered back at the house. I killed a few on the way out and escape. I've been driving around town trying to find you guys."

I nodded. My father pulled on the door but I'd already locked it.

"Don't open it," Trent muttered.

"Bryce, open the door."

I swallowed hard and looked at him carefully. Surely I could recognize if they had taken over my father. Instinctively I looked at his neck even though I knew that it wouldn't tell me anything. Once a stinger had gone into the neck, the hole closed up within a matter of hours. Skin repaired itself and unless that stinger came out of his mouth, there was no telling if he was one of them.

I placed my hand back on the handle and went to unlock it when a door opened a few houses down from where we lived. An older woman came out, she stuck her hand up and hollered to my father. It was Mrs. Holloway. Every summer my father had mowed her lawn to help her since she'd lost her husband three years go.

"Vern?"

My dad's head turned, then he looked back at me and smiled. There was something unnerving to it. But before I could determine if it was him or not, he turned and headed towards Mrs. Holloway. His neck cracked from side to side, and that's when I knew it. That wasn't him. At least he was no longer in control. There were few things that annoyed the hell out of my father, but one of them was people who cracked their neck. In all the years I'd lived with him I'd never seen him do that.

I brought the window down just a crack.

"Mrs. Holloway, get back inside," I yelled out.

"What?" She cupped a hand to her ear.

I motioned with my hand. "Get in!'

Meanwhile my father calmly walked towards the gate of her yard and unlocked it.

I unlocked my door and pushed out, then shouted again. "Get inside!"

That time she heard me. Her eyes widened, and she looked towards my father who was walking up the path that led up to her door. Now Mrs. Holloway had to have been in her early eighties. She was a dotty old woman who moved at a snail's pace. Now I don't know if she clued in, if she had seen those things tearing into other people or not, but she turned to head back inside but she was just too damn slow. Without even running towards her my father clamped his hand on the back of her dress and his head pulled back. I sprinted towards her gate with my Glock already up and both hands on it.

"Dad!"

Still holding her, he turned his head and sneered. The

stinger shot out and zeroed in on her neck. I held the gun out but couldn't shoot. I was paralyzed, completely frozen by what was occurring.

Ten, maybe twenty seconds passed, and he pulled back from her, releasing her limp body to the ground. I kept my gun out in front of me as he turned his head and I could see blood on his lower jaw. The stinger shot back into his mouth and without rushing, he stepped off a concrete step near her doorway and headed my way.

"No. Stop. I don't want to."

My hands were shaking as he came towards me. In my head I knew he wasn't in control and that I had to shoot him but I was frozen, unable to squeeze the trigger. I stumbled back, nearly falling over as he reached the gate and swung it open.

"Don't worry, son, it will all be over real soon."

"No. No!"

Right then a gun cracked, once, then twice and my father's legs buckled and he collapsed. I turned my head to see Bones standing there with his gun by his side. My heart hammered against my chest. Fear. Sorrow. A surge of emotions welled up as I looked into his eyes. Bones stepped forward with the lighter fluid.

I put out my arm. "No, wait!"

I looked back at my father. I couldn't believe this was happening. I wiped at the corner of my eye. "What if there is a way to stop them?"

He frowned. "You know as well as I do, that there is no coming back from this. Unless we set his body afire, those wounds will heal and he'll be back up on his feet again."

I thought about Anna and that damn sample. *Was Anna right? Maybe there is a way to turn back the tide and save them without severing the head or setting them ablaze?* I looked at my father, his body wasn't moving but then slowly but surely the skin around the bullet holes closed up.

"Axl," Bones said with more urgency in his voice. His hand was hovering over my father's body. *But what if there was no way?* What if Anna was wrong and the only way to stop them was to burn them? My father wouldn't have wanted to be one of them, of that I was sure.

I couldn't take the risk.

I gave a nod, turned my head and shuddered at the sound of lighter fluid being sprayed all over his body. I heard the snap of the Zippo lighter, then the whoosh of a flame igniting.

I lifted a forearm to shield my face.

And just like that, he was gone.

As flames engulfed his frame, one of those vile parasitic slugs slipped out the corner of his mouth, then another, trying to escape, trying one last desperate attempt to find another host. I scrambled away from the horrific sight as the fire consumed them.

Chapter 18

The sun was waning. I stood beside a window on the second floor of the house waiting for Axl to show. The others were downstairs. It was quiet outside, except for the odd scream. How were they picking who would die and who would turn? I thought back to the look on my brother's face, and how much fear he must have felt that night. There wasn't a damn thing I could do about it. Why didn't I go back to the house with them? I might have been able to stop them.

I heard footsteps behind me and turned to find Anna standing in the doorway.

"Any sign of them?"

"Not yet."

She came over and stood nearby looking out. "I can't believe this is happening. It seems surreal." She bit at her fingernails, nervousness showing through. "My mother used to say if the world came to an end, it wouldn't be because of a war or a hurricane but from an epidemic. A simple widespread epidemic like the flu. I didn't think it would be like this."

"And it doesn't help that there is no power."

She agreed, nodding. There was a moment of silence as both of us contemplated all that had transpired.

"Is that what you wanted to do after graduation? Become a doctor like your mother?"

"Not exactly. I was considering becoming a microbiologist, studying organisms that cause disease and so forth."

"Why that?"

She shrugged. "I already enjoyed biology and science. It seemed the most logical path to take. Besides, it's good pay, and I thought my mother would approve."

"So you got along with your parents?"

"My mother and I used to butt heads. Mostly over spending too much time in the outdoors. Strangely enough my father was the one that was most lenient. He... um... taught me about the beauty of the outdoors.

He was big into it. That's what drew him to become a park ranger. He loved being outside." She smiled sweetly. "He taught me to use a bow, start a fire without matches, fire a handgun, climb, even BASE jump."

"BASE jump? Didn't that scare the hell out of you?"

"No. Before you can BASE jump solo, you need at least two hundred skydives."

"That many?"

"Well, you could do it with no one knowing but you're taking a big risk."

I shook my head.

"What?" she asked.

"I don't know about that. I'm all for keeping my feet firmly planted on the ground."

She let out a gentle laugh. "You'd be surprised how good it feels. There is something about being up there and watching the earth racing up to meet you. It's the closest thing to having an orgasm."

"Damn. That's a high standard."

"You should try it sometime."

"Maybe I will." I paused. "I meant BASE jumping."

She smiled and gave a slow nod.

Just then several people walked by the fenced yard. They weren't running, just walking as though nothing was happening. I stepped back from the window to stay out of view. Karl had been adamant it was important to stay out of sight.

"How do they select people?"

"What do you mean?" Anna asked.

"Like how can they tell the difference between someone who has a parasite and someone who doesn't? We can't tell until the stinger shoots out. So how can they tell?"

"Does it matter?"

"Think about it. In a matter of a day they have swept through this town attacking people, turning some, killing others. If we knew how to not draw attention to ourselves, maybe we could fool them into thinking we're already infected. Then, it wouldn't matter where we went. We could survive this, at least until we could end it."

She scoffed. "End it?"

"Is it ridiculous to think we could? Hell, you wanted to be a microbiologist. Isn't that exactly how they spend their life? Trying to find cures and creating preventive measures against diseases?"

She studied me for a few seconds and then nodded. "Look, I don't think it's as easy as that. What do we know so far? The most common way for infectious diseases to spread is through direct transfer. While some bacteria and fungi are parasites, most aren't but then again we are dealing with something that is not of this world. Parasites usually enter the body by hiding in food or water but this seems to transfer like bacteria and once infected they seem to know if you are one of them or not. I don't think there is a way to fool them."

"But how do they know?"

She looked at me and shook her head. "If it truly is an alien parasite, maybe this thing is telepathic or part of a hive mind because it seems to be able to duplicate itself. Perhaps they are all controlled by one thing."

"You mean like a queen ant?"

"Yeah, essentially these things come from somewhere, right? If it's a queen and you kill that, the parasites might not die in that moment or even a day later but eventually the colony would die within a matter of a month, or maybe a year because of their life cycle."

Right then the sound of a truck's engine roaring caught our attention. Yellow headlights lit up the street, washing over the front of yards as it barreled down the road, beeping its horn.

"It's them. Let's go!"

We hurried downstairs and burst into the kitchen. "You ready?" I asked.

Karl nodded, holding an axe. Each of them had some kind of weapon, whether that was a baseball bat, a butcher's knife or garden tool. Karl pulled open the door and one by one we streamed out, heading towards the fence. I pulled back the planks of wood he'd loosened on one end and everyone crawled through and sprinted for the road where the truck was waiting.

For the first time since this had kicked off, we seemed to have luck on our side. Everyone made it to the truck and hopped into the back, filling it out. I banged on the side and Axl tore out of the street heading south on Hobbs. We hadn't even made it two blocks when Axl slammed on the brakes. Ahead, there were multiple vehicles blocking off the road and a gathering of at least thirty people. They turned our way as the truck growled. I tapped on the window and Bones slid it open.

"What do you think? Human or—"

"Hell, I'm not risking it," Axl said slamming the gearstick into reverse and jerking the wheel to the right. As the truck spun around, the group in the distance charged.

"Go!" I yelled. Smoke came off the tires as they squealed and we left behind the crowd who were in hot pursuit. Hobbs Road curled around and eventually our pursuers were out of sight. The only way south now would be via McCormick and McGill and for a few minutes we thought that would be an option.

The brakes screeched as the truck came to a halt forty feet away from another group.

"Those bastards are blocking the roads."

Axl didn't even need to be told what to do. He was now operating on pure adrenaline, the fight-or-flight instinct kicked in and he jerked the wheel and took the truck up the curb and plowed straight through a garden fence. Everyone bounced around in the truck as he took it over flower beds and through two more wood panel fences.

"If those assholes think they're smart, they have another thing coming."

The final words of a man who couldn't see beyond the next fence. The truck crashed through the wood panels and went straight into water. There was a massive splash as it nosedived, and the back shot up in the air and everyone slid down, crashing into each other and causing the truck to sink even faster. Axl had just driven us straight into a swimming pool. Water rushed in through the open windows, filling up every crevice. Amid the cries of Mrs. Parsons and the kids, Axl was yelling. It was a chaotic scene. One second we were above the water, the next swimming to the edge, soaked and scared that those who had seen us veer off were not far behind.

Ace, Bones and Trent swam to the side and climbed up onto the edge before collapsing in a puddle of heavily bleached water.

"Get up," I yelled to Bones, grabbing a hold of his jacket. There was no time to catch our breath. We all knew that group had seen us.

Karl bellowed at everyone to hurry towards the back of the house. One guy smashed the glass on the French doors. Glass shattered, and he raced inside. The others went to follow, but I grabbed a hold of Anna and shook my head. "No, this way." I shot down the side of the house, ducked through a bush into the next yard. When I turned back Bones and Axl weren't far behind. Even Trent was following. The rest had opted for the house.

It was a bad choice.

The sound of screams echoed as we hurried through

the yard and into the next one. I figured that being trapped in a house, one where the glass was already shattered, was just like inviting in trouble. There was no way we would have been able to hold them all off. Eventually they would have taken that house, and by the sounds of the screams behind us, that's exactly what had happened.

"Where the hell are you going?" Bones asked.

"Keep moving."

I knew we'd eventually have to hole up in a house as it was getting dark but entering the one with the pool wasn't smart. We squeezed, ran and climbed our way through multiple yards heading south. I had no idea where we were, but I knew avoiding the main roads was key.

As we burst through a cluster of trees, several of the branches tore at my face. I winced in agony, my lungs on fire and thighs screaming in protest. Panting hard and arriving in a cul-de-sac full of cars, I scanned the area. Axl and Bones rushed past me, and I took off again, following them until… I was blindsided.

A huge dark mass smashed into me knocking me to the pavement and causing me to roll across the ground. It hit me so hard, the machete slipped out of my grasp, clattering across stone. The assault was fast and before I knew it, I was flipped onto my side and saw a face looming over me.

I didn't even recognize who it was.

All I could do was hold them back at an arm's distance.

"Bones!" I yelled, but I got no response. I figured they were already embroiled in their own fight. The person above me was in his late forties, muscle-bound, a steroid-using freak covered in tattoos. His mouth opened, and the stinger whipped out and lunged at me. I shifted my head to the side just as it shot forward. It whipped back and then like a heat-seeking missile changed direction. This time it came within inches of my throat.

I reared back my knees striking the muscle head in the nuts, and he let out a groan. They might have had a parasite in them but they weren't invincible to being whacked in the sack. His grip eased, and I rolled him off me. I staggered away, only to trip over a fallen branch and smack my head on the ground.

What came next occurred in snapshots. Blackness crept in at the side of my eyes. I rolled trying to get up but my head was killing me. I could see the meathead rising to his feet. He staggered forward and for a minute I felt like a boxer trying to rise by the count of ten. He was ten feet away from me, then six, then four and just as he was about to pounce, an axe struck him in the side of the face. I blinked hard trying to focus and stay conscious. My head was throbbing, and my mouth filled with vomit at the sight of the blood. The sound of hacking continued for another twenty seconds, give or take, and then it stopped.

Breathing hard, I saw a figure come into view.

It wasn't Axl, Bones, Trent or even Anna.

It was Karl.

Chapter 19

Eight minutes. That's all it would have taken to get from Hobbs Street to Grand County High School by car on an ordinary day, except we were lacking wheels and this was no ordinary day. Daylight had given way to night by the time I came around. I'm not sure at what point I lost consciousness but my last memory was of Karl looming over me.

When I awoke I was alone and in an unfamiliar place.

Instinctively I reached for my neck, thinking perhaps I'd been turned into one of them and this was all part of some strange dream. I went to get up and groaned. It felt like someone had smashed me over the head with a sledgehammer.

The door opened and Anna walked in.

"Ah, you're awake."

She was holding in her hand a bowl. I looked around the room. It looked like a house. My home. My bedroom to be exact. What the heck?

"You should stay still, you took quite a knock to the head."

She sat down beside me and dabbed cloth into a bowl of water and touched my head with it. "How long have I been out?"

"Eight hours."

"Eight?"

I went to get up, and she pushed me down. "You need to stay put. Everything will be okay. In fact, this won't hurt."

"What?"

Her head tipped back and a stinger shot out of her mouth clamping down on the side of my neck. I knocked the bowl out of her hand and my eyes rolled back in my head as I felt pain course through my body.

In that moment I screamed.

And in the next breath, I awoke gasping for air.

"It's okay, it's okay, it was just a dream," Anna said. I was no longer in my bedroom but in a church. Stained-glass windows were lit up by a faint glimmer of moonlight. Axl, Bones, Trent and Karl were in different spots around the room. I backed up from Anna.

"What is it?" she asked.

"Open your mouth."

"Logan?"

"Open your mouth."

She frowned but did it. There was nothing there. My chest rose and fell rapidly. Sweat poured off my head. "I must have been having a nightmare. Where are we?"

"A community church just north of the high school."

"How the hell did I end up here?"

"I brought you here," Karl said getting up with a cigarette in his mouth and the axe in his hand. *The axe. The assailant.* It was all coming back now. "Not an easy task I might say. You ever thought about losing weight?" he said before smiling.

"How did you…?"

"Escape?" He sauntered over. "By the skin of my teeth. Had I known you guys were gonna leave us behind and go in a different direction I would have followed. I ended up climbing out of a window, the others... well, they didn't make it." He paused and looked up at a large cross on the wall as if seeking forgiveness for what he could not do for them. "I ran, not knowing where you'd all gone, that's when I heard the commotion and saw that guy attacking you."

"Oh yeah, about that," Bones piped up. "Sorry, I thought you were behind us."

Anna nodded, agreeing.

I rose to my feet and extended my hand to Karl. "You saved my life."

"And you nearly cost me mine." He took a hard toke on the cigarette. "I lost my brother back there."

"Look, I'm sorry but everything happened so quick after hitting the water. I knew heading in that house wasn't smart."

"You were right, I just wish my brother was here."

I nodded and ran a hand around the back of my head.

"Logan, you should take a seat. You took quite a

knock to that head of yours," Anna said.

The same words she used in the dream. For a second I was waiting for her head to tilt back but this time it didn't happen. I braced myself against a wooden pew and took a seat. It was a large church with carpeted floors, an aisle that split the room in two halves with fifteen pews on either side and an altar up front with tables covered in white sheets, and a large cross that took up most of the far wall. Huge oak beams loomed overhead, arching across like trees either side of a driveway. There were two large windows in the main auditorium and thick blinds covered them.

"Why are we in here?"

"Because it got too dangerous out there to keep going by foot. We will try again in two hours but this is safe, at least for now."

Axl came walking over with a can of drink and handed it to me. "It's not much but might give you some energy. You're gonna need it."

I downed it quickly and felt the hit of sugar into my

system.

Karl sat across from me. "So Anna here was telling me you guys might have a plan. A way to stop this?"

"A plan?" I looked at her. Obviously she hadn't told him everything.

"Yeah, tell us your great plan," Axl said. "I've been waiting to hear this. You see, what I don't get is out of all the things you could have grabbed when you got out of that truck, you happened to keep a hold of that damn sample. Why?"

"Because it holds the key to fighting this."

"We already know how to fight it."

"You know how to kill them inside one person but there has to be a way to wipe this out. Then maybe, just maybe those who are infected will return to normal."

Axl laughed. "Oh that is fresh. If I thought we could cure this and save those who've been infected, do you think I would have let Bones torch my old man's body?"

I screwed up my face. "Vern's dead?"

"Oh, welcome back, Matthews. In all the fun I forgot

to tell you. Let me bring you up to speed. My old man. We didn't find him. He found us. He was one of them. Yep, and after Bones here put a bullet in his head, he torched him."

"You told me to," Bones said.

"I know I did, Bones. Don't worry; I won't ride you over it. You did what I couldn't do." He got up and walked over to the altar and looked as if he was searching for something. Everyone watched him. He continued, "So, in an answer to Anna's great idea. No, I don't believe there is hope for those who are infected. What is done is done."

"But what if there is?" Anna asked.

He whirled around. "Shut up! Enough with your bullcrap. We are up shit creek without a paddle and chances are we are all going to be dead by the time morning comes. Stop filling their heads with false hope."

"Axl," I muttered. "Listen, I'm sorry about your family. We have all lost loved ones, but it will not do us any good to fight each other. You want retribution, take the war to them but the only way we will get through this, is together."

Karl laughed. "Sorry, I just had a strange flashback of you all heading one way while we went the other."

I didn't know what he wanted me to say. None of us had been in a situation like this before. Fear could drive a man to make selfish decisions in the heat of the moment. Self-preservation was a powerful thing.

"I say we get out of here. There is nothing left for us. Our parents are gone, and it's only a matter of time before they sweep through this town — hell, they are already doing it. And I for one don't think we will be able to torch the entire place."

"Maybe we won't have to," Bones said. "The government will probably do it. You heard what Vern and your gramps said about Arkansas. They contained the threat back in the '80s. They know the states that have been hit with this epidemic, who's to say they won't send out military to blow the shit out of any town within a twenty-mile radius of the impact sites."

"Are you saying there was more than one meteor site?" Karl asked.

"Seems so, prior to the CME, the solar flares caused a meteor shower. Utah wasn't the only state hit. After that an emergency broadcast was warning everyone to stay inside and telling folks that authorities had been dispatched."

"Yeah but with the blackout, I don't see that happening."

"Which means it's down to us," Anna said getting up. "We can run. Sure. But how far are we going to get if this continues to spread?"

Axl laughed. "Oh princess, I must admit I admire your spunk. You would have made one hell of a cheerleader," he said mimicking a cheerleader with invisible pompoms. "Hey, hey, are you ready to play? Say team. Go team. Humanity all the way!" He chuckled and shook his head and walked off into the back office.

"Just ignore him," I said. "Go ahead with what you were going to say."

She walked over to a chair where the Tupperware container was and picked it up. "Look at this thing. It's been out of the body for hours and it's shriveled up and formed a capsule around it, which means it relies on blood to survive."

"I don't get it, it needs blood, then how did it survive on a meteor?"

"That I'm not sure about. Remember, its alien, we are dealing with something that is far different to anything we have encountered. However, what I know about parasites from biology is that some parasites can persist in harsh conditions in a cystic form. They call it a microbial cyst. In this stage they lay dormant and can survive for a long time in a toxic environment without food or even the right temperature. When the cyst encounters a favorable environment, it can develop back into its parasitic form. Which might explain how it survived on the meteor, and why it's now no longer moving."

Bones chimed in. "Are you suggesting that thing is not

dead?"

She nodded. "At least I don't think it is. But it could be."

"Ah man, you are confusing the shit out of me," Bones said. "This is why I flunked biology."

"Anna, what is your point?" Karl asked.

"If one dies, how is it replaced? Does it need to be replaced? How are these things reproducing? Where are they coming from?"

"Outer space," Bones said.

"Oh my God." She raised a hand to her forehead. "We know that the way regular parasites on earth grow and spread is related to their life cycle. They go through different maturation stages. A brood parasite is essentially an organism that relies on hosts to raise their young. But where are these young coming from? A queen perhaps?"

"Brood parasite?"

"Yeah, you see this with some birds, insects and fish. For instance to avoid egg loss, a bird parasite will distribute its eggs among other different hosts.

This damages the host and leads to what they call an evolutionary arms race between a parasite and a host as both species coevolve."

"What? Speak English, woman," Axl said returning with a bottle of wine in his hand.

She scowled at him. "An evolutionary arms race is basically a struggle between two competing sorts of genes, traits or species, so they develop together and counter-adapt against each other."

"Okay, that is not helping," Bones said.

"To put it in a nutshell. When the genes come together, it allows the inhabited host to gain new characteristics and resistance to survive."

There was silence.

"You're telling me these things think they are doing us a favor?" I asked.

She shrugged. "Possibly. I mean let's face it. As a species we are divided. Everywhere we turn we see differences in wealth, power and status. Think about it, guys, even at an early age we develop cliques that flock together and discriminate against each other; jocks, metalheads, geeks, stoners and so on. Is it any wonder that years later we see that occur on a larger scale with belief systems, sexual preferences, gender, race, social class and so on... and before long we see people fighting each other instead of living in harmony?"

"But it's our differences that make us human," I said.

"But it's also what keeps us separate from one another," Karl added.

"Maybe this is all part of some evolutionary way to get us all on the same page. No longer at odds with one another, no longer separate. Nothing more than a means of survival."

Axl chuckled and swaggered across the church's platform singing the John Lennon song "Imagine." He was mocking her, or at least her theory on why these parasites were invading our bodies.

"You're such an asshole," she said staring at him.

"Oh princess, you should hear yourself. The world at peace? Harmony? No death? No religion? What planet are you living on? If there were hope for that, we would see it. But alas... history tells us another story — one written in blood. That makes us a fucked-up race," he said before taking a swig from the bottle of red wine. "Man, I always thought these church folks used fake wine instead of real wine for the sacrament? I guess this must be the preacher's personal stock." He took another swig. "Ah... nice. Yep, that's one thing you can always count on with us humans. We love our vices!"

"Seriously, are you drinking now?" I asked.

"Why not? We are all going to be dead by the morning. At least this way I won't feel it when that stinger hits me."

"So you're giving up?"

"Giving up? Me? No... I'm just getting with the program — it's all about harmony, isn't it, princess?"

I shook my head and turned my attention back to Anna. "Okay, so they need blood to survive, or they go dormant, that still doesn't answer the question of how these parasites were created."

"Many of them are born from eggs and then go through several stages before they find a host organism. Remember what the teacher said about mosquitoes?"

"So how do we kill them all?"

"Bug spray," Axl said before laughing.

She narrowed her gaze at him. "We stop production."

"How?"

"Find the queen and set that bitch on fire."

There was silence for a few seconds.

"Oh, and there I was thinking we were all about to get along so well," Axl said before taking another swig of wine and breaking into another out-of-tune rendition of "Imagine."

Chapter 20

"I'm sorry. I don't buy it," Axl said hopping up onto a table and swinging his legs while he pulled out a cigarette. "You want to hunt down some queen parasite. Who's saying it even exists? For all we know it could have been on another chunk of meteor, or on a different planet, and even if there was one, what makes you think killing it will help anyone? You said it yourself, when a queen of an ant colony dies, no new workers are born and the colony lives for however long their lifespan is — a few months or a year." He lit the cigarette. "For all we know these things can live forever." He sniffed and leaned back. "No, I call bullshit on your research, and I vote we leave this town ASAP — that is, if we even make it out."

"And go where?" Anna said. "If this isn't stopped, it will spread."

"It already has," I added.

There was silence as each of us chewed it over.

"He's right," Trent said referring to Axl. "As much as I would like to think there is a way to end this without taking more lives, we don't know. It's just a theory. This is an alien epidemic after all."

"More reason to head over to the school so I can run tests on this thing."

"And discover what, Anna?" Bones asked. She looked at me as if looking for moral support but I had nothing to say. As far as I was concerned this was way over my head. I just wanted to survive.

"Screw it. I'll do it myself," she snapped.

She got up and headed towards the back of the church.

"Ah, her feelings are hurt. Boohoo," Axl said in a mocking manner.

I got up and shook my head while looking at him. "Dick!" I followed her to the back of the room. She pushed through a set of doors and out into an entrance area where there were washrooms and another office.

"Hey, wait up, Anna."

She didn't look back but headed into the office. I

caught up with her as she took a seat at the desk.

"Look, they're just scared. We all are."

"And I'm not?"

I sighed. "No, I'm just saying that everyone is handling this in their own way. He's lost his father."

"I've lost both my parents, do you see me wanting to run off?" She banged her fist against the table. "My mother would have wanted me to figure this out. Find a solution."

"She would have wanted you to be safe," I said as I leaned forward. Besides, they have a point. Chances are if there was a queen, and this was part of some hive mind — it could be anywhere and we would be taking a huge risk trying to find it. No doubt it's surrounded by more of those things."

"Logan, we could be dead or one of them in a matter of hours. Wouldn't you have wanted to at least try?"

I leaned against the doorway. "I'm not saying we shouldn't try but really. What do we know about these things? Everything so far is just theory based on parasites that exist on our planet."

"I agree. And maybe that is all we have to go on, and maybe it won't be enough but I would rather die trying than keep running, hiding and living on borrowed time. This isn't just about killing one or two. It's about trying to free people, cure people."

I gave a slow nod and exhaled hard. "But what's the point in having a cure if they wouldn't take it, anyway? And don't you think that if the CDC has known about this since the '80s they would have had a cure by now, if one existed? I mean, it's their job to figure this stuff out."

She laughed. "I agree but you know how many diseases are incurable that they are still trying to find cures for? Ebola, cancer, AIDS, Alzheimer's, diabetes, asthma, malaria and dengue are just a few. Oh they have treatments, but cures, that's another thing entirely."

I chewed on the inside of my lip. "But it's possible they have a cure."

"Maybe. Maybe not."

"Anyway, I thought malaria was curable?"

"Yes. No. It's complicated. It depends on the severity and if it's diagnosed and treated promptly and correctly. All the symptoms associated with it are caused by blood stage parasites. Look, Logan, I know you are trying to help but without being able to examine that specimen, we are dealing with a bunch of unknowns. I need to get over to the school and run tests on that sample."

I gripped my head.

"You okay?" she asked.

"Yeah, I must have really rattled my brain when I hit the ground." I smiled then it faded. "By the way, I'm sorry about your parents."

She cast her gaze down and there was silence.

I continued, trying to boost her confidence. "Anna, we'll figure this out."

Right then Bones came hobbling in. "Guys, Axl is getting antsy. He's had too much to drink and wants to go and kill them."

I shook my head and went back into the sanctuary. Axl was waving around his gun and acting all erratic.

"Axl. Everything okay?"

He burst out laughing.

"Is everything okay?" He looked at Trent. "Oh you have got to love this guy. You're like a peacemaker everywhere you go. Trying to put out fires, saying the right words, doing your utmost to not let anyone down, aren't you, Matthews? Well this time you aren't going to do shit. Now I know who is responsible for this, and I will find him and fuck him up."

"What are you on about?"

He waved the barrel of his gun in front of my face, and I pushed it out of the way.

"Blake Davis and his minions."

"Axl, I think you've had too much to drink. Put the bottle down and sleep it off. We'll go later this evening to the school."

He snorted. "Oh, she convinced you, did she? Tell me, Matthews, does she give good head?"

I waved him off and turned to walk away. "You're drunk, Axl, now take a seat."

"Take a seat? Get in line. Listen up. Do you hear yourself? Are you in charge of this shit show? Huh?"

"Take a nap, we leave in an hour."

I turned to walk away, and he grabbed a hold of my jacket. "I'm heading out now, with or without you."

"No, no —"

My words caught in my throat as he pressed the barrel of the gun up against my head. "You were about to say?"

Bones walked in and hurried over. "Put it down, Axl. Now!"

"You taking his side, Bones? After all, we've been through?"

"You're not thinking clearly," Bones replied.

"Oh. Is that right?" He smiled, keeping his eyes locked on me. He breathed in deeply and then pulled his gun away. Just as I felt the cold metal leave my skin, I swung a punch, a right hook that caught him on the chin and knocked him back.

I loomed over him, jabbing my finger near his face.

"You ever point a gun at me again, you better pull the

trigger."

With that said I walked away leaving him there stunned. He groaned and muttered something about taking it easy and it was just a joke and he wouldn't have really pulled the trigger.

* * *

Two hours later, we headed out. It was pitch-black outside. We didn't have flashlights because we'd lost them when the truck nosedived in the pool. Besides our weapons, all we had were our wits, and in that moment all of us were scared.

The only upside was the location of the church. By car it would have taken only eight minutes, by foot, close to forty, but that was following the main road system. We figured we could shave off ten minutes by going out the back and jogging through the dense woodland, circling around the hospital, cutting across Williams Way and sticking to the woods until we crossed US-191.

The first leg of the journey until Walnut Lane was fine because we were shrouded by the forest, however, by the time we reached the residential area, that's when trouble reared its ugly head. Walnut Lane had a dead end that backed on to the parking lot of the hospital. Crouched down in the tree line, we were stuck on which way to go. If we double-timed it across the lot, we'd be fully exposed, and if we cut through the residential area, there was a high possibility of encountering those who'd been turned.

"Let's flip a coin," Bones said.

"Now I understand why you were caught," Trent replied, shaking his head.

From our vantage point we couldn't see any movement but that didn't mean they weren't out there prowling through the backyards of homes looking for any unsuspecting Moab residents.

"So what do you want to do?"

I was just about to speak when Axl shot out of the tree line, sprinted across Walnut Lane and ran down the street that divided the homes.

Karl frowned. "What the hell is he doing?"

We waited there for a second until he slowed up and

turned back and waved us on.

"I thought he sobered up," Trent said.

"Obviously not."

As reluctant as we all were, we burst out of the tree line running at a crouch, sticking to the shadows. When I caught up with him, I didn't have to chew him out, Trent did it for us.

"Are you really that stupid?"

"What? None of you could make up your damn minds so I decided for you."

"Yeah and you could have got us killed."

We continued on moving from house to house, sticking close to the yards and pinballing our way down the street. After making it to the mouth of the dirt road that fed into Williams Way, Trent held up a clenched hand to show that the coast was not clear and to hold. I kept my eyes on Axl as I figured if anyone would screw things up, it would be him. The smell of alcohol and cigarettes lingered on his breath.

"What we got?"

He indicated with two fingers and I peered around the thick oak. There were cops, and numerous residents farther down the road. There was a barricade of cars preventing anyone from leaving.

"You think that's them?"

"Well I can tell you for certain that there are only fifteen active officers in the Moab Police Department, and those that headed out with me were taken down."

"You survived. Maybe others did."

"No."

"How can you be sure?"

"Because one of those men over there is my partner. And believe me, I saw what happened to him. There was no escaping that."

My eyes widened. Trent turned his eyes away and stared at the ground.

"So how do we get across?" Bones asked.

"We go around."

Trent shook his head. "No, you guys have wasted enough time. This is the end of the road for me. I'll head out and create a distraction. As soon as they follow me, you guys haul ass."

My brow knit together, confusion dominating. "What?"

He explained. "I left my partner behind."

"So?" Axl piped up. "I think if he was in your shoes he would have done the same."

"I'm injured and slowing you down."

Karl pulled up close to him. "Trent, you don't need to do this."

"Yes I do."

"But what about your family?"

"They're dead. The house we went to, the one I escaped from was mine. I saw them die, and I did nothing. I was so damn scared for my life, I fled." No one said anything. We stared at him blankly. "I should have died back there."

"I told you we should have left him in the road," Axl said.

"Shut up, Axl."

"Just saying."

Trent pulled out his gun and handed it to me, along with several magazines. "Take this. You will need it."

"No, man. We can go around. Head in a different direction."

He gripped me by the shoulder. "If you guys think there is even the slightest chance, you can end this without more bloodshed, then it behooves you to find that answer. Hell, I'm going to be depending on it."

I gripped his shoulder. "You know what will happen, don't you?"

He smiled. "Kid, back at that road you could have left me there, but you didn't. You saved me, now it's my turn to repay that debt."

I shook my head. "Don't be stupid. I haven't saved shit if you run out there."

He looked off down the road. "When I was in the academy, they played us a video of a school shooting. As children were running out, two cops were running in. They paused the video on one cop heading in and told us that when we signed up our job was to run into chaos when others would go the other way. We took an oath to serve and protect and so far, I've not lived up to that."

"But—"

"No buts. When they see me and give chase, you get your asses across that road and get to that school. I'm relying on you guys to figure this out. And, Logan," he gripped my hand. "Thank you."

"For what?"

"Reminding me."

With that said he burst away from the tree line before anyone could say anything and double-timed it up the street waving his arms in the air.

"Hey! Over here!"

Trent jumped up and down and motioned for them to follow him.

The huge crowd of residents and cops turned his way and at first started walking towards him. A slow, steady pace as if they knew he wouldn't get far. That changed the moment Trent shifted direction and sprinted north

320

into the residential area. It was like watching a small group of runners taking off from the starting line. They broke off, one, two, then all of them rushing after him as he shouted, "Come on, you motherfuckers!"

The crowd disappeared behind homes, like a wave hitting the shore. I didn't even want to think about the fear he would feel when they finally caught up with him. There was no time to dwell on it.

Soon the road was clear. Our opening was here.

"Go," I said waving each of them on over to the other side of the road. Karl was first, followed by Anna and then Axl and Bones. I was the last one to head out, clutching Trent's firearm, and a sliver of hope.

Chapter 21

Bones smashed the pane of glass with his elbow, then picked away at the rest of the shards until it was safe to climb in. "That's one advantage to having no power — no alarms." He grinned as he climbed up and ducked into the school.

Glass crunched beneath our boots as we made our way into the darkened corridor.

Axl continued to dig himself a grave. "I always said the cops were a little unstable. I mean, who in their right mind sacrifices themselves?"

"Obviously not you," Anna said brushing past him. He grumbled under his breath and we pressed on. It took a while for our eyes to adjust but eventually we were able to figure out where we were.

"You know, I always wanted to have sex in school."

"Dude," Bones said.

"Just throwing it out there." Axl sniffed. "What about

you, princess?"

"I hope that wasn't a request."

"No, but if it was?"

She flipped him the bird.

"Hey come on, show Axl some love," he said.

Anna ignored him.

"Okay, so what have you always wanted to do?"

Anna was quick to answer that. "Besides punch you in the face? Um, let me see."

The rest of us cracked up laughing.

"Yeah, very funny. Come on. You must have a bucket list? Of course the odds are high that you won't be ticking any of them off, you know that trip to China or wherever the hell you want to go, but perhaps there are a few things that are possible."

We could all tell what he was getting at. Anna didn't bother to answer him. Once we found the science lab, Bones piped up. "Not to create an argument but you mentioned wanting to do some testing. How are you going to do that with no power?"

"The school has a backup generator."

"And you would know this because?" Axl asked, hopping up onto a table.

"Uh, I was here the day it kicked in when that storm took out the power lines."

"Well, some of us had more important things to do," he said pulling out his cigarettes and placing one in his mouth but not lighting it. "So where is it?" he asked with the cig hanging out.

"That's your job. Go find it."

"Me?" He removed the cigarette.

"Why, you scared?"

"Yeah right. No, I just…" He trailed off and Karl and I said we would go and find it. I gathered the two-way radios, and we took off heading towards the school basement. It was eerie being inside that school at night. At one point I thought my eyes were playing tricks on me. The light from the moon would cause shadows to dance on the walls, making it seem like someone was lurking up ahead.

"What did you do for a living, Karl?"

"I ran a B&B on the west side."

"Family?"

"No kids, but I was married."

"Was?"

He cut me a glance, and I knew not to probe any further. How many others had lost family to this? It was a like a plague that was out of control, and the worst kind. No cure. No treatment. Not even a way to see it coming. I'd always imagined if aliens invaded, people would act like mindless, emotionless beings but that was just a visual representation used in movies to invoke a reaction in the viewer. This wasn't the same. Once they took over a person's mind, their memories appeared to stay intact, it was just a different driver at the wheel. Now having said that, what Owen Davis did in the station, that wasn't human. That was… I couldn't even begin to wrap my head around what changes occurred in the body to cause a stinger to appear out of the mouth, or for hands and feet to be able to cling to walls. By all accounts it had the makings of some kind of insect but what?

"What about you? Your family, did they make it?"

My mind went back to my mother, brother and gramps. They were alive but for how long?

"Why are you doing this?" Karl asked.

"What?"

"Why don't you all get far away from here while you can?"

"Because it's our home."

"And you think she is going to be able to figure this out?"

As much as I wanted to believe that we could find some cure, I didn't think it would come from a science lab in a school in a matter of hours. But the CDC? Well maybe there was an answer to be found there, in Atlanta. We continued on down a series of steps that led into the belly of the school. It smelled like oil, and grime.

"How are we going to see anything down here?"

I pulled out a small BIC lighter and rolled my thumb over the metal spark wheel. A flame flickered to life and produced a small glow. The basement was filled with all manner of large rusted pipes that snaked away into the darkness.

"Here, use this," Karl said reaching for what appeared to be a cut-off metal pipe. He tore off some of his shirt and tied it off and we lit it to create a flaming torch. I held it out in front of us.

"This is creepy as shit down here."

We continued searching for what felt like ten minutes but it was closer to five. There were barrels of cleaning liquid, mops and buckets and an area where tools were kept. On the wall was a Playboy calendar and there was a dirty ashtray on the counter with a browned apple core surrounded by used gum.

"Over there," Karl motioned to a unit at the far side of the room. We crossed over, keeping our eyes peeled for trouble. Karl went through the process of making sure the gas generator had fuel in it before firing it up. It rumbled to life, and the lights came on. After that he searched around for a fuse panel to shut off power to all rooms except the one we'd entered.

"Can't have this place lit up like a Christmas tree."

I noticed two 30-gallon drums of gasoline lined up against the wall.

We were in the middle of making sure that the lights were off in different sections of the school by using the two-way radio. I was upstairs, he was down when the power went out.

"Karl?"

There was no answer on the other end of the line. I pressed it again, nothing came back but static. Shit, I thought as I made my way back down. I figured the generator had packed it in or he'd hit the wrong fuse. Making my way back down into the bowels of the basement, I called out to him expecting him to answer and reassure me that it was just a glitch, but I got no response. By the time I made it to the entrance of the basement, I couldn't hear a single sound.

"Karl?" I called out into the darkness before taking out the lighter and striking it. "You there?" Again nothing.

My hand moved to the Glock I'd tucked in the front of my waistband. There was a possibility he'd got a shock as the fuse panel was covered in wires and even though the generator was what was powering the school now, there was still a chance it was enough to put him on his back. I continued to call out his name as I headed in.

My stomach sank as I made my way over to where the fuse box was. It was wide open, and the two-way radio was on the floor. I tucked my gun away and picked the radio up and pressed the button on the side. It let out a squeal.

"Karl!" One more time I called out his name and then heard movement coming from the far side of the room. It was a shuffling sound like hard cloth rubbing up against metal. Following that was a groan. I hurried over, pulling the gun and holding it out while my other hand kept the flame ahead of me. As I came around a corner of the piping system, I saw him, lying on the floor ahead. I didn't even make it a few feet in when they came into view. Two of them up ahead. I recognized one as the school janitor and the other as a cook. I froze, then heard movement behind me. Turning in an instant I ducked as a hand went to grab me. I dropped the lighter, sending the entire basement into darkness, and scrambled beneath the huge water pipes that came up to waist height.

Hands reached for me as I squeezed the trigger. There was a muzzle flash, and a cry as one round hit my attacker. I continued to scramble out, hearing the other two heading in my direction. It was hard enough navigating around all the crap they had piled into the basement but now I couldn't see a damn thing. It didn't take me long to smash my knee into a stack of plastic chairs. I winced in pain but kept moving. I took cover behind a huge stack at the far side of the room and tried to stay as quiet as I could. Impossible. The dust, and rancid smell of death nearly choked me. I felt the urge to cough and tried to resist but couldn't hold it in. The second I let it out, I heard footsteps rushing towards me.

Plunged into darkness, I darted out from my hiding spot and noticed the silhouette of two figures. I squeezed off rounds but nothing hit.

The noise of the gun going off multiple times must have caught the attention of the others as within a matter of minutes, I heard Bones and Axl calling out.

"Don't come in. There's two of them," I yelled before scurrying across the floor and pushing my back up against a pipe and listening for movement. The sound of footsteps running away from me made it clear where they were heading — towards them.

That's when I made my move. I jumped up and rested my arm on top of a pipe and focused on the silhouette of one of them. Taking a deep breath I squeezed off a round and dropped him. The next crack came from a different gun — Axl's.

Then, just like that it was over.

I remained where I was for a few more seconds before threading my way back to the mouth of the basement. Lying on the floor a few feet from the stairwell were the janitor and cook. We knew if we didn't act fast, the wounds would heal and they would get back up again.

Axl gave me a hand dragging the other guy out along with Karl.

I hurried over to the gas generator and picked up the gasoline container and soaked all their bodies before taking the lighter and setting them ablaze.

The flames devoured them, burning up the infestation.

It had happened so fast. One second Karl was there, the next gone.

That was what we were all dealing with now, a danger that lurked in the shadows but walked in the day. A threat that looked like us but up close was able to end our existence.

The three of us watched their bodies burn on the concrete floor. There was nowhere for the flames to go so there was no fear of the building catching on fire. The smell of melting skin was atrocious. We didn't linger. Straight after, I powered up the generator, and we returned to the lab.

Anna was already hard at work, wearing gloves, glasses and a mask. She turned her head as we came in the door and pulled her mask down.

"Everything good?"

I shook my head. "Karl's gone."

She squeezed her eyes shut. "Shit."

"We need to speed this up. Chances are you weren't the only ones who heard those gunshots."

She pulled up her mask and continued looking under the microscope at the slug that was fully crystallized. She cut it in half and examined it.

"So what's that going to tell you?" Axl asked as he shifted his ass onto a table and gazed out a window. Bones stood by the door keeping watch on the corridor.

"We'll let's find out."

She removed one of her gloves and took a fresh scalpel and sliced a portion of her hand, then dripped droplets of blood onto the two halves of the slug. Anna stepped back and from a distance we watched. Suddenly the motionless slug came to life. Both halves devoured the small puddle of blood and then crawled their way back together again.

"Holy shit. It reformed."

Anna stepped in close and squeezed more blood onto the newly formed slug. Small tentacles shot out the sides of it sucking up the blood and within seconds it had multiplied itself so we were now looking at three of them.

"Just like I thought. It needs the blood of a host to duplicate itself but without it, it has no way to survive except in a dormant state. It works almost identical to an infectious disease. Most of the time once a parasitic organism attacks a host it multiplies and eventually interferes with the normal life functions. Symptoms show up and the host's immune system may try to respond to the parasite to destroy it. However in many cases, it overwhelms the immune system and leads to death. The question is, what is it doing to the blood cells?"

She got close, and I pulled her back. "Careful."

"I have to see. It's okay."

"Famous last words," Axl said, casting a glance over.

Anna looked at the slugs under the microscope.

"Interesting," she said as she powered on a screen that provided a close-up of the red and white blood cells.

"In English please," Axl muttered.

"Our white blood cells in our body search the blood for invading viruses, bacteria and fungi. When they find whatever is attacking our system, they go about trying to destroy the invading particle before it can cause disease. There are different white blood cells. One focuses on destroying foreign bacteria, another attacks the cell that is infected and other white blood cells deal with allergic reactions. Usually if you have a high white blood count it can indicate some kind of infection, inflammation or disease. Our bodies have around 5,000 to 10,000 white blood cells per microliter of blood. If it's showing up as less than 4,500 it's considered low, less than 1,000 and it's dangerous. In theory if we increase our white blood cell count, it will boost our immune system and fight off any invading parasite, however, that doesn't always work and we need medication. Parasites usually attack the red blood cells but this is attacking both the red and the white, preventing the body from being able to do anything."

"Hence the reason everyone changes."

"Please, tell me something I don't know," Axl said, shaking his head.

"It means there is nothing we could take that would change this. Besides killing those infected, there is only one way to get rid of this without killing the host and that is to find someone who is immune."

"Hold on a minute! What happened to let's find the queen and set that bitch on fire?"

"That was a theory, we are dealing with facts now."

Axl scoffed. "Well I hate to piss on your parade but no one is immune."

"That's what you think. We don't know for sure. What I can tell you is that some people are immune to HIV, Ebola and many other types of diseases. There was a whole study done on this since the human genome was first sequenced back in the 1990s. It was called the Resilience Project. From their research they discovered individuals who were healthy even though their genes should have caused them to be sick or in certain cases, dead. What they discovered was that certain people had white blood cells that didn't have the latch that deadly viruses use to penetrate and hijack them."

I nodded slowly. "So we just need to find someone who is immune and use their blood to create a cure?"

"That's about it," she replied.

Axl chuckled. "And I thought this would be hard."

Chapter 22

Axl hopped off the table and checked the magazine in his gun. "Well, class dismissed. I don't know about you guys but I'm getting as far away from this town as possible because statistically there is more chance of me being struck by lightning, winning the lottery multiple times and getting laid by the entire Victoria's Secret squad than there is of finding someone immune to this alien parasite," he said, his voice getting louder.

Right then, the lights flickered and then the power shut off.

"Shit. How much gas did you put in?"

"Doesn't matter, we're done now," Anna said.

"You can say that again," Bones muttered. He'd crossed over to the window and was peering out the blinds. One moment there was nothing but darkness and then several lights washed over the outside of the building. Then, engines roared, the sound of dirt bikes.

"Logan Matthews, come on down!" a voice bellowed over a megaphone mimicking the TV show *The Price Is Right*. We hurried over to the windows and peered out.

"Holy shit, they've found us."

Fanning out in different directions must have been fifty or sixty people, most of them students that we'd attended high school with, others adults, parents, folks I'd seen around town. Someone had hooked up a large floodlight, like the kind used on construction sites. Standing on top of a black truck with a megaphone in his hand was Blake Davis. Nearby were my brother Zac, my mother and gramps.

Axl paced up and down shaking the gun in his hand. "Right. What the hell do we do now?"

Bones darted across the room and stuck his head out into the corridor shifting his head from side to side.

"We get out," Anna said racing towards the door.

"No. We won't get ten feet from here. There's too many."

"Come on, don't make us come in there," Blake's

voice echoed again loudly. "You know it makes sense. Logan, I have your brother here, hell, I have all your family. Don't you want to be with them?"

"Then what do you suppose we do? I've got one magazine full of ammo, you've got two as does Bones, but that's it."

"I have a crossbow," Bones muttered, pulling off the one strapped over his back.

Axl rolled his eyes. "Listen, none of that will stop them."

I bit down on the side of my lip contemplating what to do. My mind was racing a mile a minute.

"Maybe we don't need to stop them, we just need to distract them." I paused. "Bones, give Anna the crossbow and then come with me."

"But—"

"Just give it."

He tore it off and handed it to her. At the end of it was a quiver of seven arrows. "Now Axl and Anna, you buy us some time."

"Buy you some time?" Axl asked. "Would you like me to find someone who's immune while I'm at it?" he said sarcastically as he shook his head in disbelief.

"Just do it."

I hurried out of the classroom and double-timed it down the corridor heading for the basement. My feet slipped on the waxy floor as I bolted around a corner and down the stairs. As soon as we made it to the generator, I pointed to the two 30-gallon metal barrels of gasoline I'd seen earlier near the generator. One of them was still attached to a dolly with wheels.

"Give me a hand getting this up the stairs."

"Are you serious?"

"You want to live?"

That was all that needed to be said. I rolled back the large drum to the stairs, and we heaved that puppy up as fast as we could. Once I had it on the main floor, I rolled it down to the far end of the corridor to where the main doors were and detached it from the dolly. While we were doing this, I could hear Axl shouting to them, telling them we'd found a cure and if they didn't back their shit up, Anna would go all Sigourney Weaver on them.

Once the drum was moved into place, just off to the left of the doorway, I pulled a knife and jammed it into the side causing gas to flood out. Gasoline streamed out covering the waxy floor and spilling over the steps and down into the basement.

"Okay, next one."

We hadn't even made it back down the corridor when the sound of gunshots echoed.

"Hurry."

We repeated the same process with the next barrel until we had it positioned at the other end of the corridor. "Anna!" I yelled. She stuck her head out of the classroom. I was filling up a small gasoline container from some of the liquid as it flooded out the side of the metal drum. I then handed that off to Anna and told her to douse the counters inside some of the classrooms, anything close to the windows. Bones did the same thing while I worked on a few of the rooms. The smell of gasoline filled the air as

Axl continued to fire rounds at the crowd gathered out front.

As I stepped backwards out of a classroom, dousing the floor as I went, I saw him out the corner of my eye.

"Logan."

My head turned and there in the middle of the corridor was Zac. He stood there alone. No one else with him. Startled, I dropped the small can of gasoline and reached for the Glock.

"I'm afraid, Logan."

I pulled out the gun from my waistband. "Stay back, Zac."

"Why didn't you come for me, Logan?"

Words barely escaped my lips. "I…"

"They were everywhere."

He walked towards me and I jabbed the gun outward. "Stay back."

"I'm not one of them, Logan."

Bones came out of the classroom and reacted by pulling his gun.

"Wait!" I shouted.

Bones's eyes darted between us. "Don't listen to him, Logan."

"I'm not one of them."

"How did you get in?" I asked.

"Through the window at the side of the school."

I nodded to Bones, and he headed off to check it.

He continued to walk forward. "Please, Logan."

"I'm warning you, Zac. I will squeeze the trigger."

I clenched my jaw feeling myself choking up.

"You need to believe me. I'm not one of them."

"Where's mom?"

"It's too late for her."

"Gramps?"

He shrugged and took a few more steps forward.

"I'm sorry, Zac. I'm sorry."

Just as I said that he lunged forward, his mouth opening. I saw the tip of the stinger and fired one round straight into his forehead. His body hit the ground with a thud. Anna came out of a classroom farther down the corridor; she cast her gaze at the ground and then back at me. In that instant I went numb. The world I once knew ceased to exist. It was as if I experienced that moment from outside of my body, nothing more than a spectator. I might have stayed in that comatose state if it wasn't for Bones yelling and sliding out of the door in a hurry.

"They're coming!"

He slipped on gasoline and shot across the floor into lockers before scrambling up.

"Axl, let's go!" I yelled. He backed out of the classroom firing rounds, which meant they were breaking in. "Up to the roof." Getting to the roof involved going through a skylight in the art classroom. We hurried down the corridor, and around a corner.

"Logan. Come on," Anna shouted back after noticing I wasn't going.

"No, someone needs to be here to do this. Go, I'll be there in a minute." At the far end of the corridor on either side, students and adults beat on the doors to get in. Their bodies pressed up against the doors, forcing them to bulge. Windows could be heard breaking and boots hitting the floor. My heart was hammering in my chest. Everything inside of me wanted to bolt. Fear crept up in my chest trying to choke me out for not moving. *Wait. Wait,* I told myself. Suddenly they streamed out of the classrooms, filling up the corridor and slipping in the liquid. Some piled over each other as if clamoring to be the first to taste blood. Gasoline sloshed beneath their soles as they homed in on me, their eyes filled with rage. I aimed the Glock, and without saying a word fired two rounds, one either side of me, at the floor.

There was a muzzle flash, then a whoosh as the gasoline ignited and flames swept across the floor like a tidal wave stretching back to the source. Their bodies were engulfed in tongues of fire. Screams echoed, and I turned and sprinted down the next corridor just as the flames hit the drums. Two huge explosions erupted, letting out a deafening roar and shaking the building.

My feet couldn't carry me fast enough.

I knew it had wiped out a massive number of them but

not all of them were inside or near the back doors when it exploded.

My thighs screamed, and feet pounded in a rhythm as I burst into the art room. I saw the chairs stacked on top of two tables and Bones extending a hand. I hauled ass and climbed using every last ounce of my strength.

"Logan!" a voice echoed. No sense of where it was coming from but it sounded close. I cast a glance over my shoulder but no one was there.

Bones clasped my hand and with the help of Axl, they hauled me up. I kicked away the chair at the last second and they sealed the window behind me. I was panting hard, and my strength had whittled away. All that remained was exhaustion, and pure adrenaline.

We hurried over to the far side of the roof and looked down at the carnage. Smoke poured out of the school, clouding the air and making it hard to breathe. In between the smoke I could see the black truck idling, fumes rising from its exhaust pipe. There were two people inside it. Nearby were Declan, Zane and JT on dirt bikes.

"I think we could take them," Anna said, hooking up an arrow in the crossbow. "I could take out the two in the truck, and you three can handle the others. What do you think?"

I nodded. At that stage, I was open to any ideas.

"Where's Blake?" Bones muttered.

"Hopefully dead. Let's go," I said climbing over the edge and sliding down a steel drainpipe. Once my feet hit the ground, I pulled my gun again and kept an eye out for the others. They slipped down, and we hugged the school building with our backs, staying in the shadows. Anna stayed on top of the school in a crouched position as we darted away and took cover behind a school bus.

Axl took command. "I've got JT. Bones, you take Zane and…"

"I already know," I said.

Anna gave a signal and fired. Again it was one hell of a shot, the arrow cracked the windshield and struck the guy in the driver's seat right in the face. The next shot followed less than four seconds later striking the next guy as he tried to scramble out of the vehicle.

In that instant we fanned out in combat intervals taking fire.

With the distance between and lack of practice, both of my shots missed, as did Bones's but fortunately Axl hit his target. JT collapsed on the ground, his dirt bike spinning out of control before cutting out.

Anna slid down the pipe as my eyes scanned the area, continuing to move forward and fire rounds if only to push them back so we could make it to the truck. As we came around the corner, eight Vipers remained, the rest must have been instructed to head in and had burned up in a fiery grave. As soon as they locked eyes on us, they changed direction and raced across the parking lot. Anna was coming up the side when they burst past her.

She fired off three more arrows while Axl took a knee and squeezed off a flurry of rounds. Bones headed for the truck and hauled out the dead guy from the driver's side. Axl turned to join him but was taken down by Declan who plowed into him with his bike.

I squeezed off a round and struck him in the chest as Zane came at me. His body flew off the back while his dirt bike continued on.

In those final seconds as we struggled to hold back the tide of those that remained, Anna screamed. Blake had emerged from the smoke-filled building and grabbed her by the throat. He dragged her inside, back into the darkness.

"Go!" Axl yelled, gripping his side. "I'll handle this asshole."

He turned to face Zane while I hurried back towards the school and ducked inside, keeping the lower half of my face covered with my top. I couldn't see a damn thing. Not even three feet in front of my face. The heat was intense. All around me plastic dripped and the sound of fire crackled. I dropped low to where the smoke wasn't as thick and pressed on.

The sound of Anna's scream guided me through to a classroom.

"Shut up," I heard him say. Then came a thud as if a

fist was striking a jaw.

I burst into the room, holding the gun out and focusing in on them.

"Let her go."

"Logan," he said in a condescending fashion. "I don't understand why you keep on fighting this. We're here to help you. It's better this way. Just stop resisting and you'll see. Just as your family did."

"I said..."

"Just shoot him," Anna cried.

My hand trembled. There was no way I could take the shot and be guaranteed to hit him without hitting her. But it was that or let him turn her. "See, Logan, you can't do what's needed to be done. Humanity can't do what's needed to be done. But we can. This will all be over soon." His mouth opened, and I squeezed off three rounds in rapid succession. Both of them flew backwards, slamming into a metal cabinet before crumpling to the ground and disappearing behind desks.

My pulse raced, sweat trickled down the side of my

face.

I could hear groaning but was unable to see. I moved around the tables and made my way over until they came into view. Two of the shots had left him motionless, the third had punctured her shoulder. She clutched the bloody mess and tried to move out from under the arm that was still draped over her.

"Anna." I slipped the gun into my waistband, took a knee and got close to wrap an arm around her, leaned in and went to rise when Blake's eyelids snapped open. Before I could react, the stinger shot out. I leaned forward, reaching back for the Glock just as the stinger went for her neck. Instead of sinking into her skin, it plowed into mine.

I gasped, my eyes widening as I fell back.

"You ready to die?" he croaked out. My cry caught in my throat as I raised the Glock at him and unloaded two more shots into his skull.

Anna got up and came straight over as I tried to catch my breath.

It felt like a million tiny needles were being stuck into my body, a painful sensation that was causing my body temperature to rise as if I'd stepped into boiling water.

"Logan. Logan."

I couldn't even summon a word except to hand her the gun.

She shook her head. "No. No, there has to be another way."

"Do it."

I didn't want to become one of them but I knew it was over for me.

I coughed hard feeling as if something was choking me, my eyes rolled back in my head. Through blurred vision I saw Anna set on fire Blake's body. My eyelids shut. I could hear Anna's voice bellowing near my ear — words blending together, nothing but an incoherent mass of sound echoing off my eardrum. Then, it came in clear.

"I can't do it. There has to be a way."

I reached for the gun. "Then give it to me, I'll do it."

She pulled away.

"Anna, take the shot, and burn my body."

"No, I'm gonna find a cure."

I shook my head, I'd never felt so much pain before in my life. I let out a cry and doubled over. "Go, get out of here. Now! While there is still time," I said. Tongues of fire and black smoke were engulfing every inch of the school.

She lingered, hovering over me.

I'm not sure how long she remained there, or if it was her lips I felt press against my forehead before I passed out, or even how I got outside the fiery furnace, but my last recollection was seeing her glance back at me before stepping into a truck and watching it peel away leaving a cloud of dust in its wake.

Then everything faded to black.

* * *

When I came to, it was quiet except for the sound of fire crackling and a crow cawing in the distance. Burned school papers blew across the ground like tumbleweed. The smell of death carried on the wind.

I brought a forearm up to my eyes as the sun made me squint.

My throat was dry, and my head thumped as if suffering from sun stroke.

A beautiful sunset rose on the horizon, stretching out and breathing life into everything. I had no sense of time but the memories were still there — raw and vivid. Who knew how many hours or days I'd been out, and what change had occurred inside me? I was awake, alive, and the pain was gone.

I staggered to my feet, gripping my body and taking stock of my surroundings.

I inhaled, sucking in large lungful's of air.

Was I dead?

Was this part of some strange dream?

Had I become one of them now?

Instinctively I reached up and touched my neck. There was no wound. Nothing to show that I'd been attacked or any of this was real except for the school that lay now in smoldering ruin. I opened my mouth and put two fingers deep inside and immediately felt my gag reflux kick in. No reaction. No stinger. Shouldn't it have been there?

I continued to hold my bruised and battered body as I rose and a band of warm sunlight bathed my face. I stood there for several minutes before staggering back towards town to find answers, to find someone, anyone who could verify what I now believed, what she believed — that someone was immune.

And maybe, just maybe… that was me.

Epilogue

TITAN

A WEEK LATER

If only I had known sooner.

If only we had known, more of us would be alive.

I tucked the photograph of my family into my back pocket, nothing left but memories.

Anna, Bones and Axl were out there, somewhere, that I was sure. She wouldn't give up until a cure was found. They wouldn't let up until more were dead. And now it was my job to find them. I figured they would head for the CDC in Atlanta, the one place where answers could be found, the one place she believed might hold the cure.

Except the cure wasn't out there.

It was here all along, living inside me.

My blood and DNA wasn't affected by the stinger.

How? Your guess is as good as mine but maybe Atlanta would know.

All I knew now was there was hope.

A chance for humanity to rise.

A way to turn back the tide.

So yes, I understand now.

I mean, why they did it.

Someone should keep a record — not of what happened or how few survived but as a warning to future generations. You see never could I have foreseen it ending this way, nor imagined that any of this was even possible.

Ignorance got us here; failure to act sooner was our downfall.

I don't want you to make that mistake. We can't allow it.

I recall the Sego Petroglyphs.

The questions echo in my mind.

"The Sego Petroglyph. The serpent, what does it mean?"

I had said fertility and agricultural productivity. I was wrong.

It was a warning. Arkansas wasn't the first; our ancestors had dealt with their kind before.

So here it is, my message to the world. In the event of my death these words will live on, forever etched into stone as a testament to those still fighting. If you're reading this now, just know you're not alone.

Though few, pockets of resistance still exist.

It's getting harder to know who to trust. They've adapted, evolved and become smarter but there is still hope. As long as there is breath in your lungs, never give up.

Far too many gave their lives so we can live.

This is our world, our country and our home, and we will defend it at all costs.

I scrawled furiously against the Cutler sandstone capped by harder Moenkopi sandstone and caked in a red mud curtain. The words, bright and clear, the images easier to grasp than the Sego Petroglyphs. Once done, I stepped back to admire the handiwork. Each message would tell a tale. Each engraving would paint a picture.

Not just of those who came from above, but the cure that now exists and runs through my veins.

I breathed in deeply, closed my eyes.

Nine hundred feet up in the air, standing upon the soaring fin of Titan Tower, amongst a maze of pinnacles, minarets, gargoyles, spires and strangely shaped rock formations, I soaked in the golden sunrise spreading over the towering depths of Fisher Towers in Utah.

What a beautiful sight.

This is where it all began.

It's what started it all.

The sun, the flare, the change in trajectory, and them.

A hard wind blew against my skin, I closed my eyes feeling its warmth before opening them to the world changed by evil. Though the buildings would decay, this message would remain.

I stepped up to the edge, peered over.

At one time, teetering on the edge of the unknown terrified me, but that was weeks ago, long before this, before them, before I witnessed the horror that cost so many lives. So am I scared? Of course, but this is a walk in the park compared to what lies below. One last time, I turned and moved far enough back before looking towards the horizon. I breathed in deeply before firing forward, legs pounding the ground like pistons as I hit my stride. The sound of blood rushed in my ears, the cries of the fallen tore at my heart and his words echoed as the tower fell away.

"Ready to die?"

I reply, "No, I'm ready to survive."

* * *

THANK YOU FOR READING

Book 2 will be available in October

A Plea

Thank you for reading Darkest Hour: Book 1. If you enjoyed the book, I would really appreciate it if you would consider leaving a review. Without reviews, an author's books are virtually invisible on the retail sites. It also lets me know what you liked. You can leave a review by visiting the book's page. I would greatly appreciate it. It only takes a couple of seconds.

Thank you — **Jack Hunt**

Newsletter

Thank you for buying Darkest Hour: Book 1 published by Direct Response Publishing.

Click here to receive special offers, bonus content, and news about new Jack Hunt's books. Sign up for the newsletter. http://www.jackhuntbooks.com/signup/

About the Author

Jack Hunt is the author of horror, sci-fi and post-apocalyptic novels. He currently has three books out in the War Buds Series, three in the Camp Zero series, five books out in the Renegades series, three books in the Agora Virus series, one out in the Armada series, a time travel book called Killing Time, Blackout and another called Mavericks: Hunters Moon. Jack lives on the East coast of North America.

Made in the USA
Coppell, TX
03 December 2019